James S. Burdett

Burdett's Heroic Recitations and Readings

James S. Burdett

Burdett's Heroic Recitations and Readings

ISBN/EAN: 9783337194611

Printed in Europe, USA, Canada, Australia, Japan

Cover: Foto ©Andreas Hilbeck / pixelio.de

More available books at **www.hansebooks.com**

Recitations and Readings

EDITED AND ARRANGED BY THE TALENTED

ELOCUTIONIST,

JAMES S. BURDETT.

NEW YORK:

EXCELSIOR PUBLISHING HOUSE,

29 AND 31 BEEKMAN STREET.

CONTENTS.

		PAGE
Ballad of Roland Clare, The		105
Battle of Fontenoy, The	*Thomas Davis*	5
Battle of Ivry, The	*Macaulay*	24
Battle of Morgarten, The	*Mrs. Hemans*	117
Beau	*T. H. Robertson*	73
Beth Gelert	*W. L. Spencer*	95
Bill Gibbon's Deliverance	*Arthur Matthisen*	46
Bill Mason's Bride	*Chiquita*	77
Caldwell of Springfield	*Bret Harte*	112
Charge of the Light Brigade, The	*Alfred Tennyson*	20
Christian Maiden and the Lion, The	*Francis A. Durivage*	61
Cowardly Jim	*W. A. Peters*	13
Curfew must not Ring To-Night		90
Death of " Old Braze "	*" Detroit Free Press "*	152
Defence of Lucknow, The	*Alfred Tennyson*	83
Diver, The	*Schiller*	146
Downfall of Poland, The	*Campbell*	26
Execution of Montrose, The	*Aytoun*	123
Execution of Queen Mary	*Lamartine*	87
Father John	*Peleg Arkwright*	150
Fireman, The	*Robert T. Conrad*	41
Glove and the Lions, The	*Leigh Hunt*	114
Henry of Navarre before Paris	*Nora Perry*	81
Heroism	*Hale*	7
Hervé Riel	*Robert Browning*	119
How he Saved St. Michael's	*Mary A. P. Stansbury*	92
How Jane Conquest Rang the Bell	*James Milne*	9
In the Tunnel	*Bret Harte*	128

		PAGE
Jim Bludso	*John Hay*	60
John Bartholomew's Ride	*G. H. Jennings*	44
John Maynard		22
Kate Maloney	*Geo. R. Sims*	141
Karl the Martyr		69
Last Redoubt, The	*Alfred Austin*	53
Leaguer of Lucknow, The	*James Reed*	55
Leap of Roushan Beg, The	*Henry W. Longfellow*	126
Little Hero, The	*Arthur Matthison*	97
Lochinvar	*Sir Walter Scott*	28
Main Truck, The; or, A Leap for Life	*Walter Colton*	33
Marco Bozzaris	*Fitz-Greene Halleck*	67
Martyrs of Sandomir, The		17
O'Murtogh	*Robert Buchanan*	38
Phil Blood's Leap	*Robert Buchanan*	133
Polish Boy, The	*Ann S. Stephens*	101
Ride of Jennie McNeal, The	*Will Carleton*	49
Sergeant's Story, The, of the Light Brigade		34
Seventh Fusileers, The	*Kinglake*	42
Ship on Fire, The	*Henry Bateman*	63
Spanish Armada, The	*Lord Macaulay*	79
Spanish Mother, The	*Sir Francis Hastings Doyle*	29
Supporting the Guns	*"Detroit Free Press"*	130
Tom	*Constance Fenimore Woolson*	144
Trooper's Story, The	*William Sawyer*	58
True Hero, A	*R. H. Conwell*	108

BURDETT'S

HEROIC

RECITATIONS AND READINGS.

THE BATTLE OF FONTENOY.

THRICE, at the heights of Fontenoy, the English column failed,
And twice the lines of Saint Antoine the Dutch in vain assailed ;
For town and slope were filled with fort and flanking battery,
And well they swept, the English ranks, and Dutch auxiliary.
As vainly through De Barri's wood the British soldiers burst,
The French artillery drove them back, diminished and dispersed.
The bloody Duke of Cumberland beheld with anxious eye,
And ordered up his last reserve, his latest chance to try.
On Fontenoy, on Fontenoy, how fast his generals ride !
And mustering come his chosen troops, like clouds at eventide.
Six thousand English veterans in stately column tread,
Their cannon blaze in front and flank, Lord Hay is at their head ;
Steady they step adown the slope—steady they climb the hill ;
Steady they load—steady they fire, moving right onward still,
Betwixt the wood and Fontenoy, as through a furnace blast,
Through rampart, trench and palisade, and bullets showering fast ;
And, on the open plain above, they rose, and kept their course,
With ready fire and grim resolve that mocked at hostile force.
Past Fontenoy, past Fontenoy, while thinner grow their ranks—
They break, as broke the Zuyder Zee through Holland's ocean
    banks !
More idly than the summer flies, French tirailleurs rush around,
As stubble to the lava tide, French squadrons strew the ground ;

Bomb-shell, and grape, and round shot tore, still on they marched
and fired—
Fast from each volley grenadier and voltigeur retired.
"Push on, my household cavalry!" King Louis madly cried;
To death they rush, but rude their shock—not unavenged they
died.
On through the camp the column trod—King Louis turns his
rein:
"Not yet, my liege," Saxe interposed, " the Irish troops remain ;"
And Fontenoy, famed Fontenoy, had been a Waterloo,—
Were not these exiles ready then, fresh, vehement and true?
"Lord Clare," he says, "you have your wish, there are your
Saxon foes!"
The Marshal almost smiles to see, so furiously he goes!
How fierce the look these exiles wear, who're wont to be so gay,
The treasured wrongs of fifty years are in their hearts to-day—
The treaty broken, ere the ink wherewith 'twas writ could dry,
Their plundered homes, their ruined shrines, their women's part-
ing cry,
Their priesthood hunted down like wolves, their country over-
thrown—
Each looks as if revenge for all was staked on him alone.
On Fontenoy, on Fontenoy, nor ever yet elsewhere
Rushed on to fight a nobler band than these proud exiles were.
O'Brien's voice is hoarse with joy, as, halting, he commands,
"Fix bayonets! Charge!" Like mountain storm rush on these
fiery bands!
Thin is the English column now, and faint their volleys grow,
Yet must'ring all the strength they have, they make a gallant
show.
They dress their ranks upon the hill to face that battle-wind—
Their bayonets the breakers' foam; like rocks the men behind!
One volley crashes from their line, when through the surging
smoke,
With empty guns clutched in their hands, the headlong Irish
broke.
On Fontenoy, on Fontenoy, hark to that fierce huzza!
" Revenge! remember Limerick! dash down the Sassanach!"

Like lions leaping at a fold, when mad with hunger's pang,
Right up against the English line the Irish exiles sprang;
Bright was their steel—'tis bloody now; their guns are filled with
    gore;
Through shattered ranks, and severed files, and trampled flags
    they tore;
The English strove with desperate strength, paused, rallied, stag-
    gered, fled—
The green hill-side is matted close with dying and with dead.
Across the plain, and far away, passed on that hideous wrack,
While cavalier and fantassin dash in upon their track.
On Fontenoy, on Fontenoy, like eagles in the sun,
With bloody plumes the Irish stand—the field is fought and won!

                                  Thomas Davis.

HEROISM.

THE heroic element enters largely into the world's experience, and assumes phases as various as the stages
of its history. Very different is the unflinching heroism of John Maynard, standing, with scathed eyes
and crisped hands, on the deck of a burning steamer,
and guiding her in safety amid an agony of fire, and
that of John Huss, perishing so calmly on the funeral
pyre of Constance. One was inspired duty, the other
the divinity of faith. One was the highest type of human courage, the other the grandest form of Christian
sacrifice. One was the Mecca of earthly immortality,
the other the portal of the heavenly life.

There is a heroism of patriotism. It is seen in the
bravery of a Leonidas; in the "Don't give up the ship"
of a Lawrence; in the dying words of a Warren; in
the sacrifice of the "Little Regiment;" in a Farragut
lashed to the main-top of the Hartford.

The grandest heroism, however, and that which embodies all others, is the heroism of the Cross. Its achievements are seldom noted ; its deeds and its devotion rarely told.

The last beams of the setting sun fall on the gray walls and ivy-crowned turrets of a convent, and, flashing through an open casement, light up with a tremulous glory the face of a dying nun. Her life of love, of devotion, of perfect purity, is nearly ended. No thoughts of time misspent or opportunities neglected, no recollection of cold charity, no shadow of crime, no echo of wrong, harass her last moments. Her life ebbs so peacefully, that the balmy air of evening, redolent with the perfume of flowers, and thrilling with Nature's vesper hymn, lullabies her dreamless sleep long after her ears are deaf to its melody. No minute guns, no flags at half mast, no nation in tears because her spirit has departed. Only the low sob of the organ, the solemn chant of sorrowing sisters, or, perchance, the tearful prayer of some whose pain she has soothed, whose sorrow she has cheered. Hers was an earthly mission and a heavenly reward ; and the true heroism of her life realizes its perfection when her enraptured soul thrills with the praise of the angles and the " Well done " of the Infinite.

There is also a heroism of self-sacrifice. When the life-boats were crowded so they could not hold another, the old captain stood proudly on the deck of the sinking vessel ; refused to go on board , refused to risk the lives of a score that he might save his own. "The old ship and I have weathered many a gale together, and I'll not desert her now, when she's almost

slipped her cable. So shove off, my hearties! shove
off! and if the admiral asks for me, tell him that I and
the 'Witch of the Wave' sleep breast to breast at the
bottom of Davy Jones' locker."

There is, too, a heroism of genuine devotion to
principle, sometimes akin to patriotism. Such was the
heroism of Alexander H. Stephens in his blind adher-
ence to an erring State, of Stonewall Jackson in his
idolatry of Southern rights, and of Lord Byron in his
death for struggling Greece and a lost cause.—*Hale.*

HOW JANE CONQUEST RANG THE BELL.

'TWAS about the time of Christmas, a many years ago,
When the sky was black with wrath and rack, and the earth was
    white with snow,
When loudly rang the tumult of winds and waves at strife;
In her home by the sea, with her babe on her knee, sat Harry
    Conquest's wife.
And he was on the waters, she knew not, knew not where,
For never a lip could tell of the ship to lighten her heart's de-
    spair.
And her babe was dying, dying, the pulse in the tiny wrist
Was all but still, and the brow was chill, and pale as the white
    sea mist.
Jane Conquest's heart was hopeless, she could only weep, and
    pray
That the Shepherd mild would take the child painlessly away.

The night grew deeper and deeper, and the storm had a stronger
    will,
And buried in deep and dreamless sleep lay the hamlet under the
    hill.

And the fire was dead on the hearthstone within Jane Conquest's
  room,
And still sat she with her babe on her knee, at prayer amid the
  gloom,
When, borne above the tempest, a sound fell on her ear,
Thrilling her through, for well she knew 'twas a voice of mortal
  fear.
And a light leapt in at the lattice, sudden and swift and red,
Crimsoning all the whited wall, and the floor and the roof o'er-
  head.
It shone with a radiant glory on the face of the dying child,
Like a fair first ray of the shadowless day of the land of the un-
  defiled ;   [new,
And it lit up the mother's features with a glow so strange and
That the white despair that had gathered there seemed changed
  to hope's own hue.
For one brief moment, heedless of the babe upon her knee,
With the frenzied start of a frighted heart, up to her feet rose
  she ;
And thro' the quaint old casement she looked upon the sea—
Thank God, that the sight she saw that night so rare a sight
  should be.
Hemm'd in by hungry billows, whose madness foam'd at lip,
Half a mile from the shore, or hardly more, she saw a gallant
  ship
Aflame from deck to topmast, aflame from stem to stern,
For there seemed no speck on all the wreck where the fierce fire
  did not burn.
And the night was like a sunset, and the sea like a sea of blood,
And the rocks and the shore were bathed all o'er as by some gory
  flood.
She looked and looked, till the terror crept cold thro' every limb,
And her breath came quick, and her heart turned sick, and her
  sight grew dizzy and dim,
And her lips had lost their utterance ; though she strove, she
  could not speak,
But her feeling found no channel of sound in prayer, or sob, or
  shriek.

Silent she stood and rigid, with her child to her bosom prest,
Like a woman of stone, with stiff arms thrown round a stony babe
    at breast;
Till once more that cry of anguish thrill'd thro' the tempest's
    strife,
And it stirr'd again in her heart and brain the active, thinking
    life;
And the light of an inspiration leapt to her brightened eye,
And on lip and brow was written now a purpose pure and high.
Swiftly she turn'd and softly she crossed the chamber floor,
And faltering not, in his tiny cot she laid the babe she bore;
And then, with a holy impulse, she sank to her knees and made
A lowly prayer in the silence there, and this was the prayer she
    prayed:
"Christ, who didst bear the scourging, but now dost wear the
    crown,
I at Thy feet, O true and sweet, would lay my burden down.
Thou badest me love and cherish the babe Thou gavest me,
And I have kept Thy word, nor stept aside from following Thee;
And, lo! the boy is dying, and vain is all my care,
And my burden's weight is very great! yea, greater than I can
    bear.   [lives;
And, Lord, Thou know'st what peril doth threat these poor men's
I, a lone woman, most weak and human, plead for their waiting
    wives.
Thou canst not let them perish; up, Lord, in Thy strength, and
    save
From the scorching breath of this terrible death on the cruel
    winter wave.
Take Thou my babe and watch it, no care is like to Thine,
And let Thy power, in this perilous hour, supply what lack is
    mine."

And so her prayer she ended, and rising to her feet,
Turned one look to the cradle nook where the child's faint pulses
    beat;
And then with softest footsteps retrod the chamber floor,
And noiselessly groped for the latch, and oped and crossed the
    cottage door.

The snow lay deep, and drifted as far as sight could reach,
Save where alone the dank weed strewn did mark the sloping
  beach.
But, whether 'twas land or ocean, or rock, or sand, or snow,
Or sky o'erhead, on all was shed the same fierce, fatal glow.
And thro' the tempest bravely Jane Conquest fought her way,
By snowy deep and slippery steep, to where her goal lay.
And she gain'd it, pale and breathless, and weary, and sore, and
  faint,
But with soul possess'd with the strength, and zest, and ardor of
  a saint.
Silent and weird, and lonely amid its countless graves,
Stood the old gray church on its tall rock perch, secure from the
  flood's great waves.
And beneath its sacred shadow lay the hamlet safe and still,
For howsoever the sea and the wind might be, 'twas quiet under
  the hill.
Jane Conquest reached the churchyard, and stood by the old
  church door;
But the oak was tough, and had bolts enough, and her strength
  was frail and poor.
So she crept through a narrow window and climbed the belfry
  stair,
And grasp'd the rope, sole cord of hope for the mariners in de-
  spair.
And the wild wind help'd her bravely, and she wrought with an
  earnest will,
And the clamorous bell spake out right well to the hamlet under
  the hill.
And it roused the slumb'ring fishers, nor its warning task gave
  o'er
Till a hundred fleet and eager feet were hurrying to the shore ;
And then it ceased its ringing, for the woman's work was done,
And many a boat that was now afloat showed man's work was
  begun.

But the ringer in the belfry lay motionless and cold,
With the cord of hope, the church-bell rope, still in her frozen
  hold.

How long she lay it boots not, but she woke from her swoon at
last,

In her own bright room, to find the gloom and the grief of the
peril past.

With a sense of joy within her, and the Christ's sweet presence
near,

And friends around, and the cooing sound of her babe's voice in
her ear ;

And they told her all the story, how a brave and gallant few

O'ercame each check, and reached the wreck, and saved the hapless crew ;

And how the curious sexton had climbed the belfry stair,

And of his fright, when, cold and white, he found her lying there ;

And how, when they had borne her back to her home again,

The child she left, with a heart bereft of hope, and wrung with
pain,

Was found within its cradle in a quiet slumber laid,

With a peaceful smile on its lips the while, and the wasting sick-
ness stay'd.

And she said 'twas Christ that watched it, and brought it safely
through,

And she praised His truth, and His tender ruth, who had saved
her darling too.

And then there came a letter across the surging foam,

And last the breeze that over the seas bore Harry Conquest
home.

And they told him all the story that still their children tell,

Of the fearful sight on that winter night, and the ringing of the
bell.

James Milne.

COWARDLY JIM.

IT's not much of a story, stranger,
    But what there is of it I'll tell.
We found the young chap on the prairie,
    Where he said he got lost, and, well,

It was something about the Black Hills,
    And going on foot and sich trash;
We freely remarked that, for a fellow with brains,
    We regarded him somewhat rash.

His answer was thin, too, when Johnson said,
    " P'raps you won't mind, pard, just giving a bit
Of your personal history to pass off the time."
    " As a rule of his life he'd not mention it,"
Was just what he said; but we made up our minds
    That before he'd got out of the plains
His fingers had, rather too freely,
    Stuck onto the wrong bridle-reins.

And that he had slipped the committee,
    Or something pretty much the same cut;
So he wouldn't talk out in the meeting,
    But wisely kept his under-jaw shut.
Drive him off!   Why, durn it all, stranger,
    We wern't that kind of hairpins;
When you find a man starving on the prairie,
    It's no time to talk of old sins.

We fed him just like a young baby,
    On spoon vittles and such soothing things,
Until his stomach got stronger,
    Then he tackled jerked venison, by jinks.
He hitched on the centre at camp-building time,
    For darn his picture if he'd work a bit;
But we made ourselves understood plain enough,
    By the simple remark, " You work or git."

Brown called him durned Cowardly Jim,
    And a cussed mean skunk, and all sich;
Why, not even a kick he resented
    That Jones gave him down at the ditch.
And somehow we all got to hate him,
    Till he hadn't a friend in camp,
And one day we said that at sundown
    He'd leave, or we'd hang the durned scamp.

He looked kinder lonesome and sad,
    Getting ready to leave us that night;
But some warm work in camp soon after
    Just gave him a kind of respite.
A scout had come in and said " Injuns ! "
    Well, anybody knows what that meant
Who has been down on the Rosebud
    Where Custer and his brave boys went.

Them Injuns just made our camp lively,
    And Jim, he pulled trigger with the rest,
He put in some good shots, stranger,
    Which helped send the devils back west.
But a woman rushed in all frantic,
    And said that, while hid in a trough,
The red devils ransacked the ranche,
    And had carried her baby off.

Was there a man in camp who dared
    To venture the rescue, one, or all;
Not a man, nor the whole camp would go.
    'Twas sure death to venture within shot or call
Of the Sioux with fleet ponies and fatal aim;
    But that " Cowardly Jim " just quietly said,
" If he wasn't intrudin' on any one's right,
    He'd bring back the baby alive or dead."

That stirred things in camp some, you reckon ?
    Yes, 'twas queer kind of language for Jim;
But, stranger, between me and you,
    The daringest thing on earth for him
Was to mount that little pony and go,
    As he did, and face death, as he said,
And ride where the bravest dare not ride,
    To bring back that baby alive or dead.

'Twas many a prayer that went up for Jim,
    And many a tear that fell to the ground,
As we watched him going over the hill,
    While a pin would have dropped with a sound.

And then we saw him racing for life,
  With red devils in swift pursuit ;
A riderless pony, every minute or so,
  And a puff of smoke told when Jim would shoot.

He reeled and fell from the saddle ;
  That's the blood-stained floor where he laid,
And he smiled as he said, " Here's the baby;
  Never mind the price that I paid."
We knew that his time was all up,
  Brave, noble, old Cowardly Jim.
We raised him in our arms to die,
  And, stranger, thar wus angles with him.

" My baby is waiting for me," he said,
  " At those gates of pearl, I feel ;
Husband, you wronged me ; some day you'll know
  That your Mamie was true as steel."
Why, what could he mean by all that ?
  His husband ?   Jim was out of his head.
We laid bare the bosom, and, O God !
  'Twas a woman whose life had fled !

That's her grave over there on the hill,
  Away from home, husband and all ;
" Mamie " is all we carved on it,
  And alone there she'll wait the last call.
It wasn't much of a story, stranger,
  But such as it was I have told ;
And, of all the treasure we found in the Hills,
  That heart was the purest gold.

                               W. A. Peters.

THE MARTYRS OF SANDOMIR.

THIS BEAUTIFUL POEM IS SUPPOSED TO HAVE BEEN
WRITTEN BY MONSEIGNEUR CAPEL.

SIX hundred years ago, one night,
  The monks of Sandomir
Had chanted matins in the choir,
  And then sat down to hear
The lesson from the martyrs' lives
  For the ensuing day:
For thus the Blessed Dominic
  Had taught his sons the way
To sanctify the hours that men
  In pleasure or in sleep
Are wont to spend and they took care
  His holy rule to keep.

The book lay open on the desk
  At the appointed page;
The youngest novice, who was scarce
  More than a boy in age,
Stood up to sing, and on the book
  Looked down with earnest eyes.
At once across his features stole
  A movement of surprise;
And then, with clear and steady voice,
  He sang " The Forty-nine
Martyrs of Sandomir "—and laid
  His finger on the line.
Sadoc, the Prior, almost knew
  By heart that holy book,
And, rising in his stall, he called
  With a reproving look

The novice to his side, and said,
  " My son, what hast thou sung ?
From jests within these sacred walls
  'Twere meet to keep thy tongue."

" Father," the novice answered meek,
  " The words are written all
Upon this page ; " and brought it straight
  To Sadoc in his stall.
Th' illuminated parchment shone
  With gold and colors bright,
But brighter far than all the rest,
  With an unearthly light,
Beam'd forth the words the youth had sung.
  The Prior saw the sign,
And said, " My brethren, 'tis from God ;
  Are we not forty-nine ?
It is a message from our Lord—
  Rejoice ! for by his grace,
To-morrow we shall be in Heaven,
  To-morrow see his face.
What matter if the way be hard
  And steep that leads us there ?
The time is short.   Let us make haste,
  And for our death prepare."
Then one by one at Sadoc's feet
  The monks their sins confessed
With true contrition, and rose up
  In peace, absolved and blessed.
And when the eastern sunbeams came
  In through the window tall,
Sadoc, the Prior, said Mass, and gave
  The Bread of Life to all.
      *   *   *   *   *
Like other days that wondrous day
  The holy brethren spent ;
As their rule bade them, to their meals,
  To work, to prayer they went ;

Only from time to time they said,
  "Why are the hours so long?
We thought we should have been ere now
  Joining the angels' song."
The evening came, the complin bell
  Had called them to the choir—
"God grant us all a perfect end,"
  In blessing said the Prior.

And when the complin psalms were sung,
  They chanted at the end—
"Into Thy hands, my Lord and God,
  My spirit I commend."
Again, and yet again rose up
  Those words so calm and sweet,
As when an echo from a rock
  Doth some clear note repeat.

Fierce war-cries now were heard without,
  Blows shook the convent gate:
The heathen Tartar hordes had come
  With fury filled and hate.
The brethren heeded not, nor heard
  The clamor of their foes;
For from their lips the holy hymn,
  "Salve Regina," rose.
And two and two in order rang'd
  They passed down through the nave,
And when they turned and kneeled, the Prior
  The holy water gave.
But as they sang, "O Mother dear,
  When this life's exile's o'er,
Show us the face of Christ, thy Son,"
  The Tartars burst the door.

With savage yells and shouts they came,
  With deadly weapons bare,
On murder and on plunder bent;—
  The sight that met them there,

Of that white-rob'd, undaunted band,
  Kneeling so calm and still, ,
A moment checked them in their course—
  The next, the pow'rs of ill
Had urged them on, and they began
  Their work of blood and death,
Nor stayed their hands till all the monks
  Had yielded up their breath.
So Sadoc and his brethren all
  At Sandomir were slain :
Six hundred years in Heaven have paid
  That hour of bitter pain.

Anon.

THE CHARGE OF THE LIGHT BRIGADE.

HALF a league, half a league,
Half a league onward,
All in the valley of Death,
  Rode the six hundred.
" Forward, the Light Brigade !
"Charge for the guns!" he said.
Into the valley of Death
  Rode the six hundred.

" Forward, the Light Brigade !"
Was there a man dismay'd?
Not tho' the soldiers knew
  Some one had blunder'd:
Theirs not to make reply,
Theirs not to reason why,
Theirs but to do and die.
Into the valley of Death
  Rode the six hundred.

Cannon to right of them,
Cannon to left of them,

Cannon in front of them
 Volley'd and thunder'd; ·
Storm'd at with shot and shell,
Boldly they rode and well,
 Into the jaws of Death,
Into the mouth of Hell
 Rode the six hundred.

Flash'd all their sabres bare,
Flash'd as they turn'd in air,
Sabring the gunners there,
Charging an army, while
 All the world wonder'd:
Plunged in the battery-smoke,
Right thro' the line they broke;
Cossack and Russian
Reel'd from the sabre-stroke,
 Shatter'd and sunder'd,
Then they rode back, but not,
 Not the six hundred.

Cannon to right of them,
Cannon to left of them,
Cannon behind them
 Volley'd and thunder'd;
Storm'd at with shot and shell,
While horse and hero fell,
They that had fought so well
Came thro' the jaws of Death,
Back from the mouth of Hell,
All that was left of them,
 Left of six hundred.

When can their glory fade?
Oh, the wild charge they made!
 All the world wonder'd.
Honor the charge they made!
Honor the Light Brigade!
 Noble six hundred!   *Tennyson.*

JOHN MAYNARD.

'Twas on Lake Erie's broad expanse,
  One bright midsummer day,
The gallant steamer Ocean Queen
  Swept proudly on her way.
Bright faces clustered on the deck,
  Or leaning o'er the side,
Watched carelessly the feathery foam
  That flecked the rippling tide.
Ah, who beneath that cloudless sky,
  That smiling bends serene,
Could dream that danger, awful, vast,
  Impended o'er the scene—
Could dream that ere an hour had sped,
  That frame of sturdy oak
Would sink beneath the lake's blue waves,
  Blackened with fire and smoke?
A seaman sought the captain's side,
  A moment whispered low ;
The captain's swarthy face grew pale,
  He hurried down below.
Alas, too late ! Though quick and sharp
  And clear his orders came,
No human efforts could avail
  To quench th' insidious flame.
The bad news quickly reached the deck,
  It sped from lip to lip,
And ghastly faces everywhere
  Looked from the doomed ship.
" Is there no hope—no chance of life?"
  A hundred lips implore ;
" But one," the captain made reply—
  " To run the ship on shore."

A sailor, whose heroic soul
　　That hour should yet reveal—
By name John Maynard, eastern born—
　　Stood calmly at the wheel.
" Head her south-east!" the captain shouts,
　　Above the smothered roar,
" Head her south-east without delay !
　　Make for the nearest shore ! "
No terror pales the helmsman's cheek,
　　Or clouds his dauntless eye,
As in a sailor's measured tone
　　His voice responds, " Ay, ay ! "
Three hundred souls—the steamer's freight—
　　Crowd forward wild with fear,
While at the stern the dreadful flames
　　Above the deck appear.
John Maynard watched the nearing flames,
　　But still, with steady hand
He grasped the wheel, and steadfastly
　　He steered the ship to land.
" John Maynard," with an anxious voice
　　The captain cries once more,
" Stand by the wheel five minutes yet,
　　And we will reach the shore."
Through flames and smoke that dauntless heart
　　Responded firmly still,
Unawed, though face to face with death,
　　" With God's good help I will ! "
The flames approach with giant strides,
　　They scorch his hands and brow ;
One arm disabled seeks his side,
　　Ah, he is conquered now !
But no ! his teeth are firmly set,
　　He crushes down the pain—
His knee upon the stanchion pressed,
　　He guides the ship again.
One moment yet ! one moment yet !
　　Brave heart, thy task is o'er !

The pebbles grate beneath the keel,
  The steamer touches shore.
Three hundred grateful voices rise
  In praise to God, that He
Hath saved them from the fearful fire,
  And from th' ingulfing sea.
But where is he, that helmsman bold?
  The captain saw him reel—
His nerveless hands released their task,
  He sunk beside the wheel.
The waves received his lifeless corpse,
  Blackened with smoke and fire.
God rest him !   Hero never had
  A nobler funeral pyre !

Anon.

THE BATTLE OF IVRY.

Now glory to the Lord of Hosts, from whom all glories are!
And glory to our sovereign liege, King Henry of Navarre!
Now, let there be the merry sound of music and of dance,
Through thy corn-fields green, and sunny vines, oh, pleasant land
    of France !
And thou, Rochelle, our own Rochelle, proud city of the waters,
Again let rapture light the eyes of all thy mourning daughters.
As thou wert constant in our ills, be joyous in our joy,
For cold and stiff and still are they who wrought thy walls annoy.
Hurrah ! hurrah ! a single field hath turned the chance of war.
Hurrah ! hurrah ! for Ivry, and King Henry of Navarre !
Oh, how our hearts were beating, when, at the dawn of day,
We saw the army of the League drawn out in long array;
With all its priest-led citizens, and all its rebel peers,
And Appenzel's stout infantry, and Egmont's Flemish spears.
There rode the brood of false Lorraine, the curses of our land !
And dark Mayenne was in the midst, a truncheon in his hand;

And, as we looked on them, we thought of Seine's unpurpled
    flood,
And good Coligni's hoary hair all dabbled with his blood;
And we cried unto the living Power who rules the fate of war,
To fight for His own holy name, and Henry of Navarre!
The king is come to marshal us, all in his armor drest;
And he has bound a snow-white plume upon his gallant crest.
He looked upon his people, and a tear was in his eye;
He looked upon the traitors, and his glance was stern and high.
Right graciously he smiled on us, as rolled from wing to wing,
Down all our line, a deafening shout, "Long live our lord the
    King!"
"And if my standard-bearer fall, as fall full well he may—
For never saw I promise yet of such a bloody fray—
Press where you see my white plume shine, amidst the ranks of
    war—
And be your oriflamme, to-day, the helmet of Navarre."
Hurrah! the foes are moving! Hark to the mingled din
Of fife, and steed, and trump, and drum, and roaring culverin!
The fiery Duke is speeding fast across Saint André's plain,
With all the hireling chivalry of Guelders and Almayne.
"Now, by the lips of those ye love, fair gentlemen of France,
Charge—for the golden lilies now—upon them with the lance!"
A thousand spurs are striking deep, a thousand spears in rest,
A thousand knights are pressing close behind the snow-white
    crest;
And in they burst, and on they rushed, while, like a guiding star,
Amidst the thickest carnage blazed the helmet of Navarre.
Now, Heaven be praised, the day is ours! Mayenne hath turned
    his rein,
D'Aumale hath cried for quarter. The Flemish Count is slain.
Their ranks are breaking like thin clouds before a Biscay gale;
The field is heaped with bleeding steeds and flags and cloven
    mail.
And then we thought of vengeance; and all along our van
"Remember St. Bartholomew!" was passed from man to man;
But out spoke gentle Henry, "No Frenchman is my foe;
Down, down with every foreigner, but let your brethren go."

Oh, was there ever such a knight, in friendship or in war,
As our sovereign lord, King Henry, the soldier of Navarre!
Ho! maidens of Vienna! Ho! matrons of Lucerne!
Weep, weep, and rend your hair for those who never shall return.
Ho! Philip, send for charity thy Mexican pistoles,
That Antwerp monks may sing a mass for thy poor spearmen's
      souls!
Ho! gallant nobles of the League, look that your arms be bright!
Ho! burghers of St. Genevieve, keep watch and ward to-night!
For our God hath crushed the tyrant, our God hath raised the
      slave,
And mocked the counsel of the wise, and the valor of the brave.
Then glory to His holy name, from whom all glories are;
And glory to our sovereign lord, King Henry of Navarre

Macaulay.

THE DOWNFALL OF POLAND.

OH, sacred Truth! thy triumph ceased awhile, and
Hope, thy sister, ceased with thee to smile, when
leagued Oppression poured to Northern wars her
whiskered pandours and her fierce hussars; waved
her dread standard to the breeze of morn, pealed her
loud drum, and twanged her trumpet-horn; tumultuous
horror brooded o'er her van, presaging wrath to Po-
land—and to man! Warsaw's last champion from her
heights surveyed, wide o'er the fields, a waste of ruin
laid—"Oh, heaven!" he cried, "my bleeding country
save! Is there no hand on high to shield the brave?
Yet though destruction sweep these lovely plains, rise,
fellow-men! our COUNTRY yet remains! By that dread
name, we wave the sword on high—and swear, for her
to live!—with her to die!" He said: and on the

rampart heights arrayed his trusty warriors, few, but undismayed ! firm-paced and slow, a horrid front they form, still as the breeze, but dreadful as the storm ! Low, murmuring sounds along their banners fly—RE-VENGE or DEATH ! the watchword and reply; then pealed the notes omnipotent to charm, and the loud tocsin tolled their last alarm !

In vain, alas ! in vain, ye gallant few, from rank to rank your volley'd thunder flew ! Oh, bloodiest pict-ure in the book of time, Sarmatia fell—unwept—with-out a crime ! found not a generous friend—a pitying foe—strength in her arms, nor mercy in her woe ! Dropped from her nerveless grasp the shattered spear —closed her bright eye, and curbed her high career ! Hope, for a season, bade the world farewell, and Free-dom shrieked—as KOSCIUSKO fell ! The . sun went down, nor ceased the carnage there ; tumultuous mur-der shook the midnight air—on Prague's proud arch the fires of ruin glow, his blood-dyed waters murmuring far below. The storm prevails ! the rampart yields away—bursts the wild cry of horror and dismay ! Hark ! as the smouldering piles with thunder fall, a thousand shrieks for hopeless mercy call ! Earth shook ! red meteors flashed along the sky ! and con-scious Nature shuddered at the cry !

Departed spirits of the MIGHTY DEAD ! ye that at Marathon and Leuctra bled ! Friends of the world ! restore your swords to man ; fight in his sacred cause, and lead the van ! Yet for Sarmatia's tears of blood atone, and make her arm puissant as your own ! Oh ! once again to Freedom's cause return the PATRIOT TELL—the BRUCE OF BANNOCKBURN !—*Campbell.*

LOCHINVAR.

OH, young Lochinvar is come out of the west !
Through all the wide border his steed was the best ;
And, save his good broadsword, he weapon had none ;
He rode all unarmed, and he rode all alone !
So faithful in love, and so dauntless in war,
There never was knight like the young Lochinvar !

He staid not for brake and he stopped not for stone,
He swam the Esk river where ford there was none—
But, ere he alighted at Netherby gate,
The bride had consented !—the gallant came late !—
For, a laggard in love and a dastard in war
Was to wed the fair Ellen of brave Lochinvar !

So boldly he entered the Netherby Hall,
'Mong bride's-men, and kinsmen, and brothers, and all :
Then spoke the bride's father, his hand on his sword—
For the poor, craven bridegroom said never a word—
" Oh, come ye in peace here, or come ye in war ?—
Or to dance at our bridal ?—young Lord Lochinvar ! "

" I long wooed your daughter, my suit you denied :
Love swells like the Solway, but ebbs like its tide !
And now am I come, with this lost love of mine,
To lead but one measure, drink one cup of wine !—
There are maidens in Scotland, more lovely by far,
That would gladly be bride to the young Lochinvar ! "

The bride kissed the goblet ! The knight took it up,
He quaffed off the wine and he threw down the cup !
She looked down to blush and she looked up to sigh—
With a smile on her lip and a tear in her eye.
He took her soft hand ere her mother could bar—
" Now tread we a measure ! " said young Lochinvar.

So stately his form, and so lovely her face,
That never a hall such a galliard did grace !
While her mother did fret and her father did fume,
And the bridegroom stood dangling his bonnet and plume ;
And the bride-maidens whispered, " 'Twere better by far
To have matched our fair cousin with young Lochinvar ! "

One touch to her hand and one word in her ear,
When they reached the hall door, and the charger stood near—
So light to the croupe the fair lady he swung,
So light to the saddle before her he sprung !
" She is won ! we are gone, over bank, bush, and scaur !
They'll have fleet steeds that follow ! " quoth young Lochinvar.

There was mounting 'mong Græmes of the Netherby clan :
Fosters, Fenwicks, and Musgraves, they rode and they ran.
There was racing and chasing on Cannobie Lea—
But the lost bride of Netherby ne'er did they see.
So daring in love, and so dauntless in war,
Have ye e'er heard of gallant like young Lochinvar?

Sir Walter Scott.

THE SPANISH MOTHER.

YES ! I have served that noble chief throughout his proud career,
And heard the bullets whistle past in lands both far and near—
Amidst Italian flowers, below the dark pines of the North,
Where'er the Emperor willed to pour his clouds of battle forth.

'Twas *then* a splendid sight to see, though terrible, I ween,
How his vast spirit filled and moved the wheels of the machine ;
Wide sounding leagues of sentient steel, and fires that lived to
    kill,
Were but the echo of his voice, the body of his will.

But *now* my heart is darkened with shadows that rise and fall
Between the sunlight and the ground to sadden and appall :

The woeful things both seen and done we heeded little then,
But they return, like ghosts, to shake the sleep of aged men.

The German and the Englishman were each an open foe,
And open hatred hurled us back from Russia's blinding snow ;
Intenser far, in blood-red light, like fires unquenched, remain
The dreadful deeds wrung forth by war from the brooding soul
    of Spain.

I saw a village in the hills, as silent as a dream,
Nought stirring but the summer sound of a merry mountain
    stream ;
The evening star just smiled from heaven with its quiet silver eye,
And the chestnut woods were still and calm beneath the deepen-
    ing sky.

But in that place, self-sacrificed, nor man nor beast we found,
Nor fig-tree on the sun-touched slope, nor corn upon the ground;
Each roofless hut was black with smoke, wrenched up each trail-
    ing vine,
Each path was foul with mangled meat and floods of wasted wine·

We had been marching, travel-worn, a long and burning way,
And when such welcoming we met, after that toilsome day,
The pulses in our maddened breasts were human hearts no more,
But, like the spirit of a wolf, hot on the scent of gore.

We lighted on one dying man, they slew him where he lay ;
His wife, close-clinging, from the corpse they tore and wrenched
    away ;
They thundered in her widowed ears, with frowns and curses grim,
"Food, woman—food and wine, or else we tear thee limb from
    limb."

The woman, shaking off *his* blood, rose, raven-haired and tall,
And our stern glances quailed before one sterner far than all.
"Both food and wine," she said, " I have; I meant them for the
    dead,
But ye are living still, and so let them be yours instead."

The food was brought, the wine was brought out of a secret place,
But each one paused aghast, and looked into his neighbor's face ;
Her haughty step and settled brow, and chill, indifferent mien,
Suited so strangely with the gloom and grimness of the scene.

She glided here, she glided there, before our wondering eyes,
Nor anger showed, nor shame, nor fear, nor sorrow, nor surprise ;
At every step, from soul to soul a nameless horrow ran,
And made us pale and silent as that silent murdered man.

She sat, and calmly soothed her child into a slumber sweet ;
Calmly the bright blood on the floor crawled red around our feet.
On placid fruits and bread lay soft the shadows of the win.,
And we like marble statues glared—a chill, unmoving line,

All white, all cold ; and moments thus flew by without a breath,
A company of living things where all was still—but death ;
My hair rose up from roots of ice as there unnerved I stood
And watched the only thing that stirred—the rippling of the
    blood.

That woman's voice was heard at length, it broke the solemn
    spell,
And human fear, displacing all, upon our spirits fell—
" Ho ! slayers of the sinewless ! Ho ! tramplers of the weak !
What ! shrink ye from the ghastly meats and life-bought wine ye
    seek ?

Feed and begone ! I wish to weep—I bring you out my store—
Devour it—waste it all—and then—pass and be seen no more.
Poison ! Is that your craven fear ? " She snatched a goblet up
And raised it to her queen-like head, as if to drain the cup.

But our fierce leader grasped her wrist—" No, woman ! No ! " he
    said,
" A mother's heart of love is deep—give it your child instead."
She only smiled a bitter smile—" Frenchmen, I do not shrink—
As pledge of my fidelity, behold the infant drink ! "

He fixed on hers his broad black eye, scanning the inmost soul ;
But her chill fingers trembled not as she returned the bowl.

And we with lightsome hardihood, dismissing idle care,
Sat down to eat and drink and laugh over our dainty fare.

The laugh was loud around the board, the jesting wild and light;
But *I* was fevered with the march, and drank no wine that night;
I just had filled a single cup, when through my very brain
Stung, sharper than a serpent's tooth, an infant's cry of pain.

Through all that heat of revelry, through all that boisterous cheer,
To every heart its feeble moan pierced, like a frozen spear.
" Aye," shrieked the woman, darting up, " I pray you trust again
A widow's hospitality in our unyielding Spain. '

Helpless and hopeless, by the light of God Himself I swore
To treat you as you treated *him*—that body on the floor.
Yon secret place I filled, to feel, that if ye did not spare,
The treasure of a dread revenge was ready hidden there.

A mother's love is deep, no doubt; ye did not phrase it ill,
But in your hunger ye forgot that hate is deeper still.
The Spanish woman speaks for Spain; for her butchered love,
    the wife,
To tell you that an hour is all *my* vintage leaves of life."

I cannot paint the many forms of wild despair put on,
Nor count the crowded brave who sleep under a single stone;
I can but tell you how, before that horrid hour went by,
I saw the murderess beneath the self-avengers die.

But though upon her wrenchèd limbs they leap'd like beasts of
    prey,
And with fierce hands like madmen tore the quivering life away—
Triumphant hate and joyous scorn, without a trace of pain,
Burned to the last, like sullen stars, in that haughty eye of Spain.

And often now it breaks my rest, the tumult vague and wild,
Drifting, like storm-tossed clouds, around the mother and her
    child—
While she, distinct in raiments white, stands silently the while,
And sheds through torn and bleeding hair the same unchanging
    smile.

Sir Francis Hastings Doyle.

THE MAIN TRUCK; OR, A LEAP FOR LIFE.

OLD Ironsides at anchor lay,
　　In the harbor of Mahon ;
A dead calm rested on the bay—
　　The waves to sleep had gone ;
When little Hal, the captain's son,
　　A lad both brave and good,
In sport, up shroud and rigging ran,
　　And on the main truck stood !

A shudder shot through every vein ;
　　All eyes were turned on high !
There stood the boy, with dizzy brain,
　　Between the sea and sky.
No hold had he above, below ;
　　Alone he stood in air.
To that far height none dared to go—
　　No aid could reach him there.

We gazed, but not a man could speak !
　　With horror all aghast—
In groups, with pallid brow and cheek,
　　We watched the quivering mast.
The atmosphere grew thick and hot,
　　And of a lurid hue ;
As, riveted unto the spot,
　　Stood officers and crew.

The father came on deck.　He gasped,
　　" O God ! Thy will be done ! "
Then suddenly a rifle grasped,
　　And aimed it at his son.
" Jump, far out, boy, into the wave !
　　Jump, or I fire," he said.
" That only chance your life can save ;
　　Jump, jump, boy ! "　He obeyed.

3

He sunk—he rose—he lived—he moved,
  And for the ship struck out,
On board we hailed the lad beloved
  With many a manly shout.
His father drew, in silent joy,
  Those wet arms round his neck,
And folded to his heart his boy—
  Then fainted on the deck.

Walter Colton.

THE SERGEANT'S STORY OF THE LIGHT BRIGADE.

A GRAPHIC DESCRIPTION OF THE CHARGE BY A SURVIVOR.

A SURVIVOR of the celebrated ride into the jaws of death gives, in the Boston *Commercial Bulletin*, the following graphic picture of the charge:

"Lord Cardigan's eye glanced us over; then spurring his horse forward a few paces, he said:

"'My men, we have received orders to silence that battery.'

"'My G—d!' my brother ejaculated. Then grasping my hand, he said:

"'Fred, my dear fellow, good by; we don't know what may happen. God bless you; keep close to me—'

"What more he might of said was lost in Lord Cardigan's ringing shout of:

"'Charge!'

" INTO THE JAWS OF DEATH.

" We went in at a trot ; the trot changed to a canter, and the canter into a gallop. Through the lines I could see Lord Cardigan several horse-lengths ahead riding as steadily as if he was on parade. Now, to tell the plain truth, when we had ridden a short distance, say one hundred paces, I felt terribly afraid. The truth flashed upon me in a moment that we were riding into a position that would expose us to a fire on both flanks, as well as the fire from the battery in front of us, which we had been instructed to silence. I said to myself, ' This is a ride to death ! ' but I said it loud enough for my brother to hear, and he answered and said :

" ' There goes the first ! '

" The first was Lord Lucan's aid-de-camp, Captain Nolan, who, after making a slight detour, was crossing our left to join us in the charge. A cannon-ball had just cut him in two as my brother spoke.

" My heart leaped into my mouth and I almost shrieked with fear, but I restrained myself, and setting my teeth hard I rode on. A moment later the rifle bullets from the sharpshooters on the hillside began to whistle about our ears. Saddles were empted at every step. Then came the whistling shot and the shrieking shell and tore through our squadrons, mangling men and horses, plowing bloody furrows through and through our ranks. Then my fear left me. My whole soul became filled with a thirst for revenge, and I believe the same spirit animated every man in the ranks. Their eyes flashed, and they ground their teeth and pressed closer together. The very horses caught the mad spirit, and plunged forward as if impatient to lead us to our revenge and theirs. At this time there was not much to be seen. A heavy dense smoke hung over the valley, but the flaming mouths of the guns revealed themselves to our eyes at every moment as they belched forth their murderous contents of shot and shell.

"Now a shot tore through our ranks, cutting a red line from flank to flank, then a shell plowed an oblique and bloody furrow from our right front to our left rear; anon a ricochetting shot rose over our front ranks, fell into our centre, and hewed its way to the rear making terrible havoc in its passage. Oh! that was a ride. Horses ran riderless, and men bareheaded, and splashed with the blood of their comrades pressed closer and closer and ground their teeth harder, and mentally swore a deadlier revenge as their numbers grew smaller.

" INTO THE GATES OF HELL.

"Alone and in front rode Cardigan still keeping the same distance ahead. His charger was headed for the centre of the battery. Silently we followed him. Up to this time neither my brother nor myself had received the slightest scratch, although we were now riding side by side with comrades who at the start were separated from us by several files. We reached the battery at last. Up to this time we had ridden in silence, but what a yell burst from us as we plunged in among the Russian gunners. Well would it have been for them if they had killed us all before we reached them. They had done too little and too much. They had set us on fire with passion. Only blood could quench our thirst for revenge. We passed through the battery like a whirlwind sabring the gunners on our passage. I don't believe one of them live to tell the tale of that ride. Out of the battery and into the brigade—an army it was—of cavalry. Our charge was resistless.

"The Russians fell before our sabres as corn falls before the reaper. They seemed to have no power of resistance. And there was no lack of material to work upon. They closed in upon us and surrounded us on every side, but we hewed our way through them as men hew through a virgin forest, and only stopped when we reached the bank of the Tchernaya River.

"Wheeling here, we proceeded to cut our way back again. On the return ride I was assailed by a gigantic Russian trooper who made a strike at me with his sabre. I partially guarded it, but not wholly, and the next moment felt a stinging pain in my neck. It passed in a moment, however, and I was about to make short work of the trooper, when I heard my brother cry:

"'Ah! you would, would you?' and the Russian fell cleft to the chin.

"We cut our way through and once more entered the fatal valley. When half way back to our starting point a cannon shot struck my brother and beheaded him. Tom, ah, thank you!"

The color-sergeant drained another glass.

"When we formed up on arriving at our starting point, Lord Cardigan, with the tears streaming from his eyes, said:

" ' It was not my fault, my men.'

" And the men replied with one voice :

" ' We are ready to go in again, my lord, if you will lead us.'

" Just then I became dizzy. My scalp had been lifted by the stroke of the Russian's sabre, the skin of my cheek cleft across to my upper lip, and I fainted from loss of blood.

" When my time expired in the cavalry I re-enlisted in this regiment. I am always proud to hear myself called one of the six hundred, but—poor Jack ! fill that glass again, Tom."

Thus ended the sergeant's story of the famous charge.—*Anon.*

O'MURTOGH.

To-night we drink but a sorrowful cup—
  Hush ! Silence ! and fill your glasses up.
Christ be with us ! Hold out and say :
  " Here's to the Boy that died this day !"

Wasn't he bold as the boldest here ?
  Red coat or black did he ever fear ?
With the bite and the drop, too, ever free !
  He died like a man—I was there to see !

The gallows was black, our cheeks were white,
  All underneath in the morning light ;
The bell ceased tolling swift as thought,
  And out the murdered Boy was brought.

There he stood in the daylight dim,
  With a priest on either side of him ;

Each priest look'd white as he held his book,
   But the man between had a brighter look !

Over the faces below his feet
   His gray eye gleam'd so keen and fleet :
He saw us looking; he smiled his last—
   He couldn't wave, he was pinioned fast.

This was more than one could bear,
   For the wench who loved him was with us there ;
She stood in the rain with her dripping shawl
   Over her head, for to see it all.

But when she met the Boy's last look,
   Her lips went white, she turned and shook ;
She didn't scream, she didn't groan,
   But down she dropt as dead as stone.

He saw the stir in the crowd beneath,
   And I saw him tremble and set his teeth ;
But the hangman came with a knavish grace,
   And drew the nightcap over his face.

Then I saw the priests, who still stood near,
   Pray faster and faster to hide their fear :
They closed their eyes, I closed mine too,
   And the deed was over before I knew.

The crowd that stood all round of me
   Gave one dark plunge like a troubled sea ;
And I knew by that the deed was done,
   And I opened my eyes and saw the sun.

The gallows was black, the sun was white,
   There he hung, half hid from sight ;
The sport was over, the talk grew loud,
   And they sold their wares to the mighty crowd.

We walked away with our hearts full sore,
   And we met a hawker before a door.
With a string of papers an arm's-length long,
   A dying speech and a gallows song.

It bade all people of poor estate
  Beware of O'Murtogh's evil fate;
It told how in old Ireland's name
  He had done red murther and come to shame.

Never a word was sung or said
  Of the murdered mother, a ditch her bed;
Who died with her new-born babe that night,
  While the blessed cabin was burning bright.

Nought was said of the years of pain;
  The starving stomach, the dizzy brain:
The years of sorrow, and want and toil,
  And the murdering rent for the bit of soil.

Nothing was said of the murther done,
  On man and woman, and little one;
Of the bitter sorrow and daily smart,
  Till he put cold lead in the factor's heart.

But many a word had the speech beside :——
  How he repented before he died;
How, brought to sense by the sad event,
  He prayed for the Queen and the Parliament!

What did we do, and mighty quick,
  But tickle the hawker's brains with a stick;
And to pieces small we tore his flam,
  And left him quiet as any lamb!

Pass round your glasses!   Now lift them up!
  Powers above! tis a bitter cup!
Christ be with us!   Hold out and say,
  " Here's to the Boy that died this day!"

Here's his health!—for bold he died;
  Here's his health!—and it's drunk in pride.
The finest sight beneath the sky
  Is to see how bravely a MAN can die.
                              Robert Buchanan.

THE FIREMAN.

THE city slumbers. O'er its mighty walls
Night's dusky mantle soft and silent falls;
Sleep o'er the world slow waves its wand of lead,
And ready torpors wrap each sinking head.
Stilled is the stir of labor and of life,
Hushed is the hum, and tranquillized the strife.
Man is at rest, with all his hopes and fears;
The young forget their sports, the old their cares;
The grave are careless; those who joy or weep
All rest contented on the arm of sleep.

Sweet is the pillowed rest of beauty now,
And slumber smiles upon her tranquil brow!
Her bright dreams lead her to the moonlit tide,
Her heart's own partner wandering by her side;
'Tis summer's eve; the soft gales scarcely rouse
The low-voiced ripple and the rustling boughs;
And, faint and far, some minstrel's melting tone
Breathes to her heart a music like its own.

When, hark! Oh, horror! what a crash is there!
What shriek is that which fills the midnight air?
'Tis fire! 'tis fire! She wakes to dream no more,
The hot blast rushes through the blazing door;
The dun smoke eddies round, and, hark! that cry;
" Help! help! Will no one aid? I die, I die! "
She seeks the casement; shuddering at its height
She turns again; the fierce flames mock her flight;
Along the crackling stairs they fiercely play,
And roar, exulting, as they seize their prey.
" Help! help! Will no one come? " She can no more,
But, pale and breathless, sinks upon the floor.

Will no one save thee? Yes, there yet is one
Remains to save, when hope itself is gone;

When all have fled, when all but he would fly,
The fireman comes, to rescue or to die.
He mounts the stair—it wavers 'neath his tread;
He seeks the room, flames flashing round his head;
He bursts the door; he lifts her prostrate frame,
And turns again to brave the raging flame.
The fire-blast smites him with its stifling breath;
The falling timbers menace him with death;
The sinking floors his hurried step betray,
And ruin crashes round his desperate way;
Hot smoke obscures, ten thousand cinders rise,
Yet still he staggers forward with his prize,
He leaps from burning stair to stair.   On! on!
Courage!   One effort more, and all is won!
The stair is passed—the blazing hall is braved;
Still on! yet on! once more!   *Thank Heaven, she's saved!*
                              Robert T. Conrad.

THE SEVENTH FUSILEERS.

On the extreme left of Codington's brigade, at the
battle of the Alma, were posted the Seventh Fusileers.
The commander of this regiment was a man of onward,
fiery temper, named Lacy Yea.   This Lacy Yea was so
rough an enforcer of discipline, that he had never
been much liked by those who had to obey him; but
when once the Seventh Fusileers were in campaign,
and, still more, when they came to be engaged with the
enemy, they found that their Colonel was a man who
could and would seize for his regiment such chances of
welfare and of glory as might come with the fortunes of
war; and not many months were over before they
learned that, though other regiments might be dying of

want, yet, by force of their Colonel's strong will, there was food and warmth for the Seventh Fusileers.

On the morning of the battle there suddenly rose up a murmur which, coming from men of Teuton blood, was the advent of a new and seemingly extrinsic power. From the left of the line to the first company of the Seventh Fusileers, the deep, angry, gathering sound was: " Forward! Forward! Forward!" And the English, springing up the hill-side, halted upon the summit.

Lacy Yea and his men had scarcely taken up their position when the great Valdemir column, detaching itself from the corps of the Grand Duke Michael, began to move slowly down upon the English line. Before it confuses itself by hasty firing, a Russian column, in good order, is a solemn expression of warlike strength. With the hard, upright outline of a wall, it is, in its color, a dark cloud; and the lowly beings who compose it are so merged in the grand unity of the mass, that, in the hour of battle, the aspect of it weighs heavy upon the imagination of anxious men. More, a hundred fold more than it *is*, it seems to portend.

Suddenly the Valdemir column halted, and delivered a fire that threw the line of the regiment into confusion. Lacy Yea knew that his men, in order to fight, must keep in line; and what man could do he did. His very shoulders so labored and strove, with the might of his desire, to form the line, that the curt, red shell jacket he wore was as though it were a world too scant for the strength of the man and the passion that raged within him. But when he turned, his dark eyes yielded fire; and all the while, from his deep-chiselled, merciless lips, there pealed the thunder of imprecation and command.

Wherever the men had become clustered together, there, fiercely coming, he wedged his way into the thick of the crowd, and by force of will tore it asunder and formed it into line.

Presently the fire of the Fusileers began to injure the symmetry of the spruce Russian column. Lacy Yea observed that every now and then, when a part of the column was becoming faulty, a certain man, of vast towering stature, would stride quickly up to the defective spot, and exert so great an ascendency that order was always restored ; that this man was to the Russian column, what the Colonel was to the Seventh : and it was not, I think, without a sort of sympathy for him that Lacy Yea ordered his soldiers to shoot the tall man. He was obeyed.   Instantly the straight, rigid Russian ranks became bent and wavy ; then the mass became fluid, and the outlines of what had been like a wall became like the outlines of a cloud.   First some, then more, then all turned about.   Moving slowly, and as discontented with its fate, the Valdemir column began to retreat.   Lacy Yea and his Seventh Fusileers had won the day.—*Kinglake.*

JOHN BARTHOLOMEW'S RIDE.

A California Incident.

I ARN'T very much "on the fancy,"
    And all sich sort of stuff—
For an engineer on a railroad
    Is more apt "to be on the rough ;"

He don't "go much" on "his handsome,"
  I'm free to "acknowledge the corn;"
But he has to "get up" on his "wide-awake,"
  " That's just as sure's you're born."

Now, I'll tell you a little story
  'Bout "a run" we made for our necks.
When we thought "Old Gabe" had called us
  To ante up our checks.
We came round the curve by the tunnel,
  Just beyond the American Flat—
When my fireman sings out, " Johnny!
  Look ahead! my God, what's that?"

You bet! I warn't long in sightin'—
  There was plenty for me to see,
With that train full of kids and wimmen,
  And their lives all hangin' on me—
For the tunnel was roarin' and blazin',
  All ragin' with fire and smoke,
And " Number Six" close behind us—
  Quick, sonny! shove in the coke!

" Whistle down-breaks," I first thought—
  Then thinks I, " Old boy," twon't do—
And with hand on "throttle" and " lever,"
  I knew I must "roll 'em through"—
Through the grim mouth of the tunnel—
  Through smoke and flame as well
Right into the "gateway of death," boys
  Right smack through "the jaws of hell."

The staunch " Old Gal" felt the pressure
  Of steam through her iron joints—
She acted just like she was human
  Just like she knew "all the points;"
She glinted along the tramway
  With speed of a lightning flash
With a howl assuring us safety,
  Regardless of wreck or crash.

Now, I s'pose I might have jumped the train,
  In hope to save sinew and bone
And left them wimmen and children
  To take that ride alone,
Put I thought cf a day of reck'nin'
  And whatever "Old John's" done here,
No Lord ain't goin' to say to him then,
  "You went back as an engineer!"

                                    G. H. Jennings.

BILL GIBBON'S DELIVERANCE.

NEVER heerd tell of o' Bill Gibbon?
  Why, yer've kinder bin out of existence!
I don't believe some on you'd think,   ˙
  If it warn't for a little assistance.

I aint "over smart"—not myself?
  Well, you said I was—what's it matter!
To know Bill was, I guess, kinder cute,
  So let's have no more o' that chatter.

What did he do? Well—I'm darn'd!
  If yer won't, pretty soon, raise my dander!
For yer ought to know Bill just as well
  As the geese on a pond knows the gander!

Wall, there! yer needn't get riled!
  Smooth your feathers back, steady, I'll tell, mates—
Tell yer one of his feats in the woods,
  A braver deed never befell, mates!

In Wisconsin's big forests, one day,
  We was makin' a clearin' in fall time;
And the thing as Bill Gibbon done then
  I, for one, shall remember for all time.

A broad-shoulder'd coon was old Bill,
    With a will, like his muscles, of iron;
He'd a tackled a buffalo bull,
    And at choppin'—well, warn't he a spry 'un!

It was choppin' as brought it about, boys,
    For Bill had begun on a whopper,
A two-hundred foot mighty pine,
    As was doom'd to sure death by his chopper!

We'd all on us stopp'd,—work was done;
    He'd finish, "dog-gorn'd, if he wouldn't!"
An' we quit him, all full of our chaff,
    An' laughin' and sayin' he couldn't!

He buried his axe in the tree;
    We set off for our cabin, us others;
" I'll kill him afore eight!" he cries,
    " Him and p'raps one or two of his brothers!"

On the floor of his hut "afore eight"
    He lay, and he told us all, gasping,
How it happ'd—his voice broken and hoarse,
    His rough, big brown hand my own grasping.

Fast and strong fell his strokes on the tree
    It sway'd, an' it creak'd, an' it quiver'd
It toppled, it fell!—then says he
    As he spoke, why we all on us shiver'd.—

" I struck the last blow with such force
    That the tree in a second was timber,
And I fell to the earth just as stiff
    As the minute before I'd been limber.

" Swoop upon me the giant tree crash'd!
    Fiercely fell on my right leg and broke it!
An' it seemed to shriek out for revenge—
    Revenge! just as if it had spoke it.

" Help! I cried, but a long hour had gone
    Since I'd seen you boys homewards all file off,
And a bugle's voice wouldn't bin heard
    In them thick woods and bushes a mile off.

" I couldn't lie there all the night,
    So I made up my mind in a second—
I know'd as the leg must come off,
    So, to do it myself best, I reckon'd.

" One stroke!—what was left of the leg
    Was freed from the tree and its branches ! "
And what poor Bill Gibbon then said,
    Why, the thought of it now my cheek blanches.

My heart knocks aloud at my ribs,
    Though I aint in the leastways white-liver'd,
When I think what he did on that night,—
    By his right hand how he was deliver'd !

He tried, with a pluck all his own,
    To crawl, inch by inch, to his cabin ;
Though each move as he made on the road
    Was, we'd most on us think, just like stabbin'.

When he found as he couldn't get on,
    Because his two legs wasn't equal,
A bold thought comes into his head,
    As you'll see when I tell you the sequel.

A word and a blow 'twas with Bill—
    He'd act on a thought soon as catch it—
His right leg was off, his axe gleam'd,
    And he cut off his left leg to match it.

He sturdily stump'd to his hut,
    A glass of hot rum quick we mixes ;
Overcome, there's not one of us speaks
    As his torn limbs we splices and fixes !

" A stout constitooshun ! "   Well, yes !
 A hero, too, birth, bone and breeding,—
What's that you say, you out there,
 How he did fur to stop all the bleeding?

Oh, didn't I mention—that's odd !—
 'Bout them limbs as was torn into ribbons?
Wal, yer see, didn't matter to him,
 'They was wooden legs, mates, was Bill Gibbon's ! "

        Arthur Matthison.

THE RIDE OF JENNIE M'NEAL.

PAUL REVERE was a rider bold—
Well has his valorous deed been told ;
Sheridan's ride was a glorious one—
Often it has been dwelt upon.
But why should men do all the deeds
On which the love of a patriot feeds?
Hearken to me, while I reveal
The dashing ride of Jennie M'Neal :

On a spot as pretty as might be found
In the dangerous length of the Neutral Ground,
In a cottage, cosy, and all their own,
She and her mother lived alone.
Safe were the two, with their frugal store,
From all of the many who passed their door;
For Jennie's mother was strange to fears,
And Jennie was large for fifteen years ;
And while the friends who knew her well
The sweetness of her heart could tell,
A gun that hung on the kitchen wall
Looked solemnly quick to heed her call ;
And they who were evil-minded knew
Her nerve was strong, and her aim was true.

4

So all kind words and acts did deal
To generous, black-eyed Jennie M'Neal.

One night, when the sun had crept to bed,
And rain-clouds lingered overhead,
Close after a knock at the outer door,
There entered a dozen dragoons or more
Their red coats, stained by the muddy road,
That they were British soldiers showed;
The captain his hostess bent to greet,
Saying: " Madam, please give us a bit to eat;
We will pay you well, and, if may be,
This bright-eyed girl for pouring our tea;
Then we must dash ten miles ahead,
To catch a rebel colonel abed.
He visited home, as doth appear;
We will make his pleasure cost him dear."
And they fell on the hasty supper with zeal.
Close-watched the while by Jennie M'Neal.

For the gray-haired colonel they hovered near
Had been her true friend, kind and dear;
And oft, in her younger days, had he
Right proudly perched her upon his knee,
And told her stories, many a one,
Concerning the French war, lately done.
She had hunted by his fatherly side,
He had shown her how to fence and ride;
And once had said: " The time may be,
Your skill and courage may stand by me."
So sorrow for him she could but feel,
Brave, grateful-hearted Jennie M'Neal.

With never a thought or a moment more,
Bare-headed she slipped from the cottage door,
Ran out where the horses were left to feed,
Unhitched and mounted the captain's steed,
And down the hilly and rock-strewn way
She urged the fiery horse of gray.

Around her slender and cloakless form
Pattered and moaned the ceaseless storm;
Secure and tight, a gloveless hand
Grasps the reins with stern command;
And full and black her long hair streamed,
Whenever the ragged lightning gleamed.
And on she rushed for the colonel's weal,
Brave, lioness-hearted Jennie M'Neal.

Hark! from the hills, a moment mute,
Came a clatter of hoofs in hot pursuit;
And a cry from the foremost trooper said:
" Halt! or your blood be on your head!"
She heeded it not, and not in vain
She lashed the horse with the bridle-rein,
So into the night the gray horse strode;
His shoes hewed fire from the rocky road;
And the high-born courage that never dies
Flashed from his rider's coal-black eyes.
The pebbles flew from the fearful race,
The rain-drops grasped at her glowing face.
" On, on, brave beast!" with loud appeal,
Cried eager, resolute Jennie M'Neal.

" Halt!" once more came the voice of dread;
" Halt! or your blood be on your head!"
Then, no one answering to the calls,
Sped after her a volley of balls.
They passed her in her rapid flight,
They screamed to her left, they screamed to her right;
But, rushing still o'er the slippery track,
She sent no token of answer back,
Except a silvery laughter-peal,
Brave, merry-hearted Jennie M'Neal.

So on she rushed, at her own good will,
Through wood and valley, o'er plain and hill;
The gray horse did his duty well,
Till all at once he stumbled and fell,

Himself escaping the nets of harm,
But flinging the girl with a broken arm.
Still, undismayed by the numbing pain,
She clung to the horse's bridle-rein,
And gently bidding him to stand,
Petted him with her able hand;
Then sprung again to the saddle-bow
And shouted: " One more trial now ! "
As if ashamed of the heedless fall,
He gathered his strength once more for all,
And galloping down a hill-side steep,
Gained on the troopers at every leap;
No more the high-bred steed did reel,
But ran his best for Jennie M'Neal.

They were a furlong behind, or more,
When the girl burst through the colonel's door,
Her poor arm helpless, hanging with pain,
And she all drabbled and drenched with rain,
But her cheeks as red as firebrands are,
And her eyes as bright as a blazing star,
And shouted; " Quick! be quick, I say;
They come! they come! Away! away! "
Then sunk on the rude white floor of deal,
Poor, brave, exhausted Jennie M'Neal.

The startled colonel sprung, and pressed
The wife and children to his breast,
And turned away from his fireside bright,
And glided into the stormy night;
Then soon and safely made his way
To where the patriot army lay;
But first he bent in the dim firelight,
And kissed the forehead broad and white,
And blessed the girl who had ridden so well,
To keep him out of a prison-cell.
The girl roused up at the martial din,
Just as the troopers came rushing in,

And laughed, e'en in the midst of a moan,
Saying, " Good sirs, your bird has flown.
'Tis I who have scared him from his nest;
So deal with me now as you think best."
But the grand young captain bowed, and said :
" Never you hold a moment's dread.
Of womankind I must crown you queen;
So brave a girl I have never seen.
Wear this gold ring as your valor's due,
And when peace comes I will come for you."
But Jennie's face an arch smile wore,
As she said : " There's a lad in Putnam's corps,
Who told me the same, long time ago ;
You two would never agree, I know.
I promised my love to be true as steel,"
Said good, sure-hearted Jennie M'Neal.

Will Carleton.

THE LAST REDOUBT.

KACELYEVO's slope still felt
The cannons' bolts and the rifles pelt;
For the last redoubt up the hill remained,
By the Russ yet held, by the Turk not gained.

Mehemet Ali stroked his beard;
His lips were clinched and his look was weird;
Round him were ranks of his ragged folk,
Their faces blackened with blood and smoke.

"Clear me the Muscovite out !" he cried.
Then the name of " Allah !" echoed wide,
And the fezzes were waved and the bayonets lowered,
And on to the last redoubt they poured.

One fell, and a second quickly stopped
The gap that he left when he reeled and dropped;

The second—a third straight filled his place;
The third—and a fourth kept up the race.

Many a fez in the mud was crushed,
Many a throat that cheered was hushed,
Many a heart that sought the crest
Found Allah's arms and an houri's breast.

Over their corpses the living sprang,
And the ridge with their musket-rattle rang,
Till the faces that lined the last redoubt
Could see their faces and hear their shout.

In the redoubt a fair form towered,
That cheered up the brave and chid the coward;
Brandishing blade with a gallant air,
His head erect and his bosom bare.

"Fly! they are on us!" his men implored,
But he waved them on with his waving sword.
"It cannot be held; 'tis no shame to go!"
But he stood with his face set hard to the foe.

Then clung they about him, and tugged, and knelt.
He drew a pistol from out his belt,
And fired it blank at the first that set
Foot on the edge of the parapet.

Over, that first one toppled; but on
Clambered the rest till their bayonets shone,
As hurriedly fled his men dismayed,
Not a bayonet's length from the length of his blade.

"Yield!" but aloft his steel he flashed,
And down on their steel it ringing clashed;
Then back he reeled with a bladeless hilt,
His honor full, but his life-blood spilt.

They lifted him up from the dabbled ground;
His limbs were shapely, and soft, and round.
No down on his lip, on his cheek no shade—
"Bismillah!" they cried; "'tis an Infidel maid!"

Mehemet Ali came and saw
The riddled breast and the tender jaw.
" Make her a bier of your arms," he said.
" And daintily bury this dainty dead !

Make her a grave where she stood and fell,
'Gainst the jackal's scratch and the vulture's smell.
Did the Muscovite men like their maidens fight,
In their lines we had scarcely supped to-night."

So a deeper trench 'mong the trenches there
Was dug for the form as brave as fair ;
And none, till the Judgment trump and shout,
Shall drive her out of the Last Redoubt.

Alfred Austin.

THE LEAGUER OF LUCKNOW.

WITH the few whom fate of battle left and pestilence had spared,
To Lucknow's shattered fortalice the Brigadier repaired.
No bugle sounded cheerily, no drum beat the chamade,
But like a funeral cortege were those wearied files arrayed.
A cloud rests on each sun-burnt brow, gloom lowers in every eye,
But each heart is honor's goblet, and with valor brimming high.
" Soldiers ! your courage must not droop, your manly spirits
      wane ;
The stoutest bark afloat may drive before the hurricane ;
Reverses are true manhood's test ! " thus spoke in accents clear,
To his scant but brave associates, the undaunted Brigadier.
" I charge you by the mercy that ye hope to win above,
And by the distant homes where dwell the mothers that ye love,
By the sisters ye would shelter from dishonor's blighting touch,
On peril of your souls, guard sacred from pollution's touch
Yon true devoted heroines ! As ye are men this day !
By the manes of the brave who died in this accursed fray,
And by the far-off green churchyards wherein your fathers rest ;
And that home-love, which but with life forsakes the wanderer's
      breast,

And by the Queen whose throne ye guard, whose fame ye hold so
   dear,
Protect them whilst a man remains!" cried the stout old Briga-
   dier.
" Enough for human feeling.   Now for sterner work, my sons!
To your posts, and ply your rifles! lay the mortars! serve the
   guns!
Though our foes for leagues extended, like unnumbered locusts
   lie,
And ye have barely space to fight—there's room enough to die!
But let no shot be wasted ; every ball must find its man!
When yon recreant caitiff rebels, traitor-hounds of Hindostan,
All remorseless as the tiger from his sweltering jungle-fen,
Rush from under their defenses, let there be no wavering then!"
Now shook the earth, now shakes the sky, and blackness palls the
   sun,
And lightning-flames stream glaring out from many a well-laid
   gun ;
And now the mine's volcano bursts its dark concealment sheer,
And rock'd and sway'd the ramparts round the stout old Briga-
   dier.
As upward on the tortured air the scathing meteors gush,
Ten thousand sable mutineers from tower and temple rush ;
On, on they come! and the lava flame is their fitting ambuscade ;
But 'tis on to doom! and that fiery gloom is Fate's beseeming
   shade.
The red flames slack, the smoke rolls back—the swarthy bands
   appear,
And a hail-storm falls from the leaguered walls, and strikes them
   down like deer.
All day, as 'twere a brazen vault, the sky seems molten red,
And scarred and black the scorching soil reels underneath their
   tread ;
Yet own those noble hearts so tried no thought of yielding fear ;
" Bravo! well done, bold comrades!" cries the stout old Briga-
   adier.
Ladies of England's castle halls, fair as the dew-gemmed flowers
That deck in fragile loveliness your safely-guarded bowers,

Bright-eyed maids of Ireland's valleys, loving-hearted as you're
    fair,
Ask ye why those nameless heroes fought and bled and perished
    there ?
Daughters of Scotland's cottage homes, sweet as the spring-day
    morn,
Ye sunbright joys to manly hearts that sorrow else had torn,
Needs there to you repeat the tale of blood and lurid shame ?
Or needs there ask from you the meed of honor and of fame
For heroes whose keen weapons knew neither ruth nor rest,
Till every point was bent or broken in a murderer's breast ?
A sacred zeal inspires each heart for vengeance, sharp and dire
As Retribution's angel ever flung from hand of fire,
For CAWNPORE's day of nameless shames, and agony and fear,
Aye, till the earthworks crumbled round the stout old Brigadier.
Three months of ceaseless battle in that burning cordon's fold;
Three months upon the verge of fate within that leaguered hold ;
Hope of rescue lost and faded, hope of life itself departed,
Still allegiance paid to duty, not a threatened post deserted,
Peril shunned or danger shrunk from, by the worn, but golden-
    hearted ! |ance
Heaven ! and is there, then, no succor ? not a ray-light of assur-
For such unmatched resolution, such unquenchable endurance ?
Has all on duty's gory shrine been sacrificed in vain—
Famine and burning thirst endured, and fever's racking pain ?
And must they die unaided, and, such dreadful ordeal passed,
Must the ruins they defended be their sepulchre at last,
And none be left to tell the tale of bravery and woe ?
Farewell, then, gallant countrymen ! No ! by the round world,
    no !
Hark ! booming in the distance, sweet as Hope's angelic lyre,
A sound comes sailing like a note from Mercy's smiling choir !
To the God in heaven be praise ! for yon gun's reverb'ing voice,
Bids the weary sleep in safety, and the mourning souls rejoice.
Now the thunder's diapason grows more resonant and strong,
And the rifle's intonation bears a burden to its song!
Noble HAVELOCK advances ! See his conquering banners wave !
Oh, smile again, ye gentle ones ! bear up awhile, ye brave !

Lo! breasting the war-surges, like a stout ship on the main,
With the CAMPBELL he is coming!   There's redemption in their
    train!
Heaven help the strong deliverers! see their nimble rifles flash,
As with slogan-shout triumphantly from post to post they dash—
Hurrah! the last stockade is shivered, and with high exulting
    cheer,
They clasp their rescued comrades, and the stout old Brigadier!

James Reed.

THE TROOPER'S STORY.

Do I plead guilty to it?   Yes, I do,
    For I have never lied, and shall not now;
But give me a dog's leave to say a word
    Touching what happened, and the why and how.

The night-guard went their round that night at one;
    My post was in the lower dungeon range,
Down level with the moat, all slime and ooze
    And damp; but there, 'tis fit we change and change,

We sentinels.   Besides, 'twas in a sort
    The place of honor, or of trust, we'll say,
For in the cell there with the mortised door
    The young boy-lord, guilty of treason, lay.

Well, with my partisan I'd tramped an hour
    Down in the dark there—just a lantern hung
By the wet wall—when close at hand I heard
    My own name spoken by a woman's tongue.

My hair was like to lift my morion up,
    For the keep's haunted; but I turned to see
A woman like a ghost—white face, all white,
    Ready to drop, and not a yard from me.

How she had come there, God in Heaven knows.
   However, long before my tongue I'd found,
She tore out of her hair, the white pearls, big
   As pigeon's eggs, and then dropp'd to the ground.

" One word ! " she said, " only one word with him.
   He dies to-morrow ! See ! my pearls I give ;
My bracelets, too ! " She slipp'd them from her arms ;
   " One word, and I will bless you while I live.

" Your face is stern. O ! but one word, one word ! "
   With my big hand I set her on her feet ;
But she clung to me ; would not be thrust off,
   Still pleading in a bird's voice, soft and sweet.

" Only one word with him ! " that was her plea ;
   " One word ; he would be dead at break of day ; "
She wept till all her pretty face was wet,
   And my heart melted ; yea, she had her way.

They spoke together. Did I hear ? Not I.
   Best ask me if I took her bribes. Well, there,
You know the rest ; know how yon Judas spy,
   Yon starveling cur, crawled down the winding stairs.

And how he caught the bird fast in the cage,
   And made report of me with eager breath,
For breach of duty. Right, it was a breach,
   And that means, in our soldier fashion, death !

Well, I can face it ; I'm no craven hound,
   Like yonder Judas spy. Nay, had I leave
To slit his weasand for him, as I'd slice
   An onion, I'd meet death and never grieve.
                             William Sawyer.

JIM BLUDSO.

WALL, no! I can't tell where he lives,
  Because he don't live, you see:
Leastways, he's got out of the habit
  Of livin' like you and me.
Whar have you been for the last three years,
  That you haven't heard folks tell
How Jimmy Bludso passed in his checks,
  The night of the " Prairie Belle "?

He warn't no saint—them engineers
  Is all pretty much alike—
One wife in Natchez-under-the-Hill,
  And another one here, in Pike.
A careless man in his talk was Jim,
  And an awkward man in a row—
But he never pinked, and he never lied,
  I reckon he never knowed how.

And this was all the religion he had—
  To treat his engine well;
Never be passed on the river;
  To mind the pilot's bell;
And if ever the " Prairie Belle " took fire,
  A thousand times he swore
He'd hold her nozzle agin the bank
  Till the last soul got ashore.

All boats has their day on the Mississip',
  And her day came at last—
The Movastar was a better boat,
  But the Belle, she wouldn't be passed,
And so came tearin' along that night,
  The oldest craft on the line,
With a nigger squat on her safety-valve,
  And her furnaces crammed, rosin and pine.

The fire bust out as she clared the bar,
  And burnt a hole in the night,
And quick as a flash she turned, and made
  For that willer-bank on the right.
There was runnin' and cursin', but Jim yelled out
  Over all the infernal roar,
" I'll hold her nozzle agin the bank
  Till the last galoot's ashore."

Thro' the hot, black breath of the burnin' boat
  Jim Bludso's voice was heard,
And they all had trust in his cussedness,
  And know'd he would keep his word.
And sure's you're born, they all got off
  Afore the smoke-stacks fell,
And Bludso's ghost went up alone
  In the smoke of the " Prairie Belle."

He warn't no saint—but at judgment
  I'd run my chance with Jim
'Longside of some pious gentlemen
  That wouldn't shook hands with him.
He'd seen his duty a dead sure thing,
  And went for it thar and then ;
And Christ ain't a-goin' to be too hard
  On a man that died for men.

John Hay.

THE CHRISTIAN MAIDEN AND THE LION.

" GIVE the Christians to the lions!" was the savage Roman's
    cry,
And the vestal virgins added their voices shrill and high,
And the Cæsar gave the order, " Loose the lions from their den !
For Rome must have a spectacle worthy of gods and men."

Forth to the broad arena a little band was led,
But words forbear to utter how the sinless blood was shed.
No sigh the victims proffered, but now and then a prayer
From lips of age and lips of youth rose upward on the air;
And the savage Cæsar muttered, " By Hercules! I swear,
Braver than gladiators these dogs of Christians are."

Then a lictor bending slavishly, saluting with his axe,
Said, " Mighty Imperator! the sport one feature lacks:
We have an Afric lion, savage, and great of limb
Fasting since yestereven; is the Grecian maid for him?"

The Emperor assented.   With a frantic roar and bound,
The monster, bursting from his den, gazed terribly around,
And toward him moved a maiden, slowly, but yet serene;
" By Venus!" cried the Emperor, " she walketh like a queen."

Unconscious of the myriad eyes she crossed the blood-soaked
     sand,
Till face to face the maid and beast in opposition stand;
The daughter of Athene, in white arrayed, and fair,
Gazed on the monster's lowered brow, and breathed a silent
     prayer.
Then forth she drew a crucifix and held it high in air.

Lo, and behold! a miracle! the lion's fury fled,
And at the Christian maiden's feet he laid his lordly head,
While as she fearlessly caressed, he slowly rose, and then,
With one soft, backward look at her, retreated to his den.
One shout rose from the multitude, tossed like a stormy sea:
" The Gods have so decreed it; let the Grecian maid go free!"

Within the catacombs that night a saint with snowy hair
Folded upon his aged breast his daughter young and fair;
And the gathered brethren lift a chant of praise and prayer;
From the monster of the desert, from the heathen fierce and wild,
God has restored to love and life his sinless, trusting child.

Francis A. Durivage.

THE SHIP ON FIRE.

MORNING! all speedeth well; the bright sun
Lights up the deep blue wave, and favoring breeze
Fills the white sails, while o'er that Southern Sea
The ship, with all the busy life within,
Holds on her ocean course, alone, but glad!
For all is yet, as all has been, the while
Since the white cliffs were left, without or fear
Or danger to those hundred grouping now
Upon the sunny deck.
        Fire! Fire! Fire! Fire!

Scorching smoke in many a wreath,
  Sulphurous blasts of heated air;
Grim presentiment of quick death,
  Crouching fear and stern despair—
Hist! to what the master saith:
  "Steady, steersman; steady there!" Ay! ay!

To the deck the women led,
  Children helped by stalwart men;
Calmly, firmly mustered,
  All the crew assembled then,
And to order briefly said,
  Comes the sharp response again: Ay! ay!

"To the masthead!" It is done;
  "Look to leeward!" Scores obey;
"And to windward!" Many a one
  Turns and never turns away;
Steadfast is the word and tone—
  "Man the boats and clear away!" Ay! ay!

Hotter! hotter! heave and strain,
  In the hollow, on the wave,
Pump and flood the deck again.
  Work, no danger daunts the brave:

Hope and trust are not in vain,
  God looks on and He can save   **Ay! ay !**

Desolate ! All desolate !
  Nothing, nothing to be seen ;
Wait and watch and hope and wait,
  Hope has never hopeless been ;
" Men, ye know that God is great ;
  Would He, He can intervene." **Ay ! ay !**

" What above ? " Nor sail, nor sound
  " Leeward ? " Nothing far or near ;
" What to windward ? " To the bound
  Of the horizon all is clear ;
Yet again the words go round—
  " Work, men, work ; we dare not fear ! " **Ay ! ay !**

From a heavy lurch, a beam,
  Struggling, shivering, reeling back—
Crash ! with rush and shout and scream
  Comes the foreyard with its wrack,
Crushing hope, as it might seem—
  " Steady ! keep the sunline track ! " **Ay ! ay !**

All is order ! ready all !
  Watching in appointed place
Underneath the sunny pall ;
  Firm of foot, with tranquil face,
Resolute, whate'er befall,
  Holds the captain's measured pace. **Ay ! ay !**

Hotter, hotter, hotter still !
  Backward driven every one ;
All in vain the various skill ;
  All that man can do is done ;
" Brave hearts ! strive yet with a will,
  Never deem that hope is gone." **Ay ! ay !**

Hist ! as if a sudden thought
  Dare not utter what it knew,

Falls a trembling whisper, fraught
   As of hope, to frighten few ;
With a doubting heart-ache caught,
   And a choking, " Is it true ? " Ay ! ay !

There comes " A sail ! a sail ! "
   Up from prostrate misery,
Up from heart-break, woe and wail,
   Up to shuddering ecstasy ;
" Can so strange a promise fail ?
Call the master, let him see ! " Ay ! ay !
     Silence ! Silence ! Silence ! Pray !

Every moment is an hour,
   Minutes long as weary years,
While, with concentrated power,
   Through the haze that clear eye peers—
" No—yes—no "—the strong men cower
   Till he sighs—faith conquering fears—Ay ! ay !

Riseth now the throbbing cry,
   Born of hope and hopelessness ;
Iron men weep bitterly,
   Unused hands and cheeks caress ;
Feelings, wild variety,
   Strange and heartless were it less. Ay ! ay !

Through the sunlight's glittering gleam,
   On old ocean's rugged breast,
As a fantasy in dream ;
   Yet beyond all doubt confessed,
Comes the ship—God's gift they deem—
   Ah, " He overruleth best ! " Ay ! ay !

Coming ! Comes ! that foremost man
   Shouts, as only true heart may,
" Ship on fire ! You will ? You can ?
   Near us for the rescue, stay ! "
Almost as the words began,
   Answering words are on their way—Ay ! ay !

5

"Ay! ay!" words of little worth
  But as imaging the soul;
See, the boats are struggling forth;
  Marvel how they pitch and roll
On the dark wave, through the froth;
  God can bring them safe and whole.   Ay! ay!

Have a care, men! have a care!
  Steady, steady to the stern!
Now, my brave hearts, handy there;
  See, the deck begins to burn!
Child and woman, soft and fair,
  Go; thank God; be quick; return.   Ay! ay!

Blistering smoke, all dim and red,
  Writhing flakes of lurid flame;
Decks that scorch the hasty tread;
  Shuddering sounds, as if they came
Wailing from a tortured bed;
  Boatswain, call each man by name.   Ay! ay!

Strong, sad, now, one by one,
  At the voice which all obey;
Silently, till all are gone,
  Fill the boats and pass away,
And the captain stands alone;
  Has he not done well the day?   Ay! ay!

Oh, that boat-load! anxious eyes,
  Hearts where painful throbbings dwell,
Wait and watch with sympathies
  Far too deep for tongue to tell,
All suppressed are words and cries,
  Surely it will go all well!   Ay! ay!

All is well! that man so true
  Stands upon a stranger deck,
And a thrilling pulse runs through
  Those glad hearts which none may check;
Listen to the wild halloo,
  Rainbow-joy in fortune's wreck.   Ay! ay!

Pah! a rush of smothered light
  Bursts the staggering ship asunder;
Lightnings flash, fierce and bright,
  Blasting sounds, as if of thunder.
Dread destruction wins the fight,
  Round about, above and under. Ay! ay!

Come away, we may not stay,
  All is done that man can do;
Let us take our onward way,
  Life has claims and duties new;
God is a strong help and true,
  He will guide our pathway through. Ay! ay!

Thanks unceasing! thanks and praise
  For the great deliverance shown;
May the remnant of our days
  Testify what He has done;
Marvellous are His loving ways,
  Merciful, as we have known! Ay! ay!

And so the good ship Merchantman sailed on,
  With double freight of life and God's kind care,
Till at the Cape her rescued voyagers
  Left to the other kindness of the dwellers there,
She spread her sails again and went her way.
                Henry Bateman.

MARCO BOZZARIS.

AT midnight, in his guarded tent,
  The Turk lay dreaming of the hour
When Greece, her knee in suppliance bent,
  Should tremble at his power;
In dreams, through camp and court he bore
The trophies of a conqueror;
  In dreams his song of triumph heard;

Then wore his monarch's signet ring—
Then pressed that monarch's throne—a king !
As wild his thoughts and gay of wing
  As Eden's garden bird.

An hour passed on—the Turk awoke-
  That bright dream was his last;
He woke—to hear his sentry's shriek,
    "To arms! they come! the Greek! the Greek!"
He woke—to die, midst flame and smoke,
And shout, and groan, and sabre-stroke,
  And death-shots falling thick and fast
As lightnings from the mountain cloud;
And heard, with voice as trumpet loud,
  Bozzaris cheer his band—
"Strike till the last armed foe expires !
Strike for your altars and your fires !
Strike for the green graves of your sires !
  God, and your native land!"

They fought like brave men, long and well;
  They piled that ground with Moslem slain;
They conquered—but Bozzaris fell,
  Bleeding at every vein.
His few surviving comrades saw
His smile when rung their proud hurrah,
  And the red field was won;
Then saw in death his eyelids close
Calmly as to a night's repose,
  Like flowers at set of sun.

Come to the bridal chamber, Death !
  Come to the mother, when she feels,
For the first time, her first-born's breath;
  Come when the blessed seals
That close the pestilence are broke,
And crowded-cities wail its stroke;
Come in Consumption's ghastly form,
The earthquake's shock, the ocean's storm ;

Come when the heart beats high and warm,
  With banquet song, and dance, and wine,
And thou art terrible ; the tear,
The groan, the knell, the pall, the bier,
And all we know, or dream, or fear
  Of agony, are thine !

But to the hero, when his sword
  Has won the battle for the free,
Thy voice sounds like a prophet's word,
And in its hollow tones are heard
  The thanks of millions yet to be.
Bozzaris ! with the storied brave
  Greece nurtured in her glory's time,
Rest thee—there is no prouder grave
  Even in her own proud clime.
  We tell thy doom without a sigh ;
For thou art Freedom's now, and Fame's—
One of the few, the immortal names,
  That were not born to die.

                                Fitz-Greene Halleck.

KARL THE MARTYR.

It was the closing of a summer's day,
And trellis'd branches from encircling trees
Threw silver shadows o'er the golden space
Where groups of merry-hearted sons of toil
Were met to celebrate a village feast,
Casting away, in frolic sport, the cares
That ever press and crowd and leave their mark
Upon the brows of all whose bread is earned
By daily labor. 'Twas, perchance, the feast
Of fav'rite saint, or anniversary
Of one of bounteous Nature's season gifts
To grateful husbandry—no matter what
The cause of their uniting. Joy beamed forth

On ev'ry face, and the sweet echoes rang
With sounds of honest mirth, too rarely heard
In the vast workshop man has made his world,
Where months of toil must pay one day of song.

Somewhat apart from the assembled throng
There sat a swarthy giant, with a face
So nobly grand, that though (unlike the rest)
He wore nor festal garb nor laughing mien,
Yet was he study for the painter's art.
He joined not in their sports, but rather seemed
To please his eye with sight of others' joy.
There was a cast of sorrow on his brow,
As though it had been early there.   He sat
In listless attitude, yet not devoid
Of gentlest grace, as down his stalwart form
He bent, to catch the playful whisperings
And note the movements of a bright-haired child
Who danced before him in the evening sun,
Holding a tiny brother by the hand.
He was the village smith (the rolled-up sleeves
And the well-charred leathern apron showed his craft),
Karl was his name, a man beloved by all.

He was not of the district.   He had come
Amongst them ere his forehead bore one trace
Of age or suffering.   A wife and child
He had brought with him; but the wife was dead.
Not so the child, who danced before him now
And held a tiny brother by the hand—
Their mother's last and priceless legacy !
So Karl was happy still that these two lived,
And laughed and danced before him in the sun.

The frolics pause : now Caspar's laughing head
Rests wearily against his father's knee
In trusting lovingness : while Trüdchen runs
To snatch a hasty kiss (the little man,
It may be, wonders if the tiny hand
With which he strives to reach his father's neck

Will ever grow so big and brown as that
He sees imbedded in his sister's curls) ;
When quick as lightning's flash up starts the smith,
Huddles the frightened children in his arms,
Thrusts them far back, extends his giant frame,
And covers them as with Goliath's shield.

Now hark ! a rushing, yelping, panting sound,
So terrible that all stood chilled with fear ;
And in the midst of that late joyous throng
Leapt an infuriate hound, with flaming eyes,
Half-open mouth, and fiercely bristling hair,
Proving that madness drove the brute to death.
One spring from Karl, and the wild thing was seized
Fast prison'd in the stalwart Vulcan's gripe.
A sharp, shrill cry of agony from Karl
Was mingled with the hound's low fevered growl,
And all, with horror, saw the creature's teeth
Fixed in the blacksmith's shoulder.   None had power
To rescue him ; for scarcely could you count
A moment's space ere both had disappeared—
The man and dog.   The smith had leapt a fence,
And gained the forest with a frantic rush,
Bearing the hideous mischief in his arms.

A long receding cry came on the ear,
Showing how swift their flight, and fainter grew
The sound.   Ere well a man had time to think
What might be done for help, the sound was hushed—
Lost in the very distance ; women crouched
And huddled up their children in their arms,
Men flew to seek their weapons-—'twas a change
So swift and fearful none could realize
Its actual horrors for a time : but now,
The panic past, to rescue and pursuit.

Crash through the brake into the forest track ;
But pitchy darkness, caused by closing night
And foliage dense, impedes the avengers' way,
When lo ! they trip o'er something in their path—

It was the bleeding body of the hound,
Warm, but quite dead.   No other trace of Karl
Was near at hand; they called his name in vain,
They sought him in the forest all night through—
Living or dead he was not to be found.

At break of day they left the fruitless search.
Next morning, as an anxious village group
Stood meditating plans what best to do,
Came little Trüdchen, who, in simple tones,
Said, " Father's at the forge, I heard him there
Working long hours ago, but he is angry,
I raised the latch, he bade me to begone.
What have I done to make him chide me so ? "
And then her bright blue eyes ran o'er with tears.
" The child's been dreaming through this troubled night,"
Said a kind dame, and drew the child towards her ;
But the sad answers of the girl were such
As led them all to seek her father's forge.
It lay beyond the village some short span ;
They forced the door, and there beheld the smith.
His sinewy frame was drawn to its full height,
And round his loins a double chain of iron,
Wrought with true workman skill, was riveted
Fast to an anvil of enormous weight.
He stood as pale and statue-like as death.
Now let his own words close the hapless tale.

" I killed the hound, you know, but not until
His maddening venom through my veins had passed ;
I know full well the death in store for me,
And would not answer when you called my name,
But crouched among the brushwood while I thought
Over some plan.   I know my giant strength,
And dare not trust it after reason's loss ;
Why, I might turn and rend whom most I love.
I've made all fast now.   'Tis a hideous death.
I thought to plunge me in the deep, still pool
That skirts the forest, to avoid it ; but

I thought that for the suicide's poor shift
I would not throw away my chance of heaven,
And meeting one who made earth heaven to me.
So I came home and forged these chains about me—
Full well I know no human hand can rend them—
And now am safe from harming those I love.
Keep off, good friends!   Should God prolong my life,
Throw me such food as nature may require ;
Look to my babes : *this* you are bound to do ;
For by my deadly grasp on that poor hound
How many of you have I saved from death
Such as *I* now await?   But hence, away !
The poison works !   These chains must try their strength ;
My brain's on fire !   With me 'twill soon be night."

Too true his words ; the brave, great-hearted Karl—
A raving maniac—battled with his chains
For three fierce days.   The fourth day saw him free—
For Death's strong hand had loosed the martyr's bonds.

Anon.

BEAU.

(Dedicated to the Modern " Heroic " School of Writers.)

HON. PONDEROUS POLYLOQUENT, LOQUITUR.

THAT reminds me, dear sir, of a little occurence which happened
        When I was a lad.
Ah, let me replenish your glass, sir.   And if you'll permit me,
        I shall be very glad
To recount it to you, for I venture to flatter myself that
        It is other than bad.

You observe, at the side table there, that majestic old darky
        Well, that, sir, is Beau,

The hero who made himself famous upon that occasion,
      A long time ago,
'Way back in Virginia—let's see, if my memory serves me,
      In the year twenty-fo'.

'Twas in Albemarle County, Virginia, my father resided
      Till the day that he died;
Well off in fine horses, and niggers, and arable acres,
      And family pride;
Thomas Jefferson's friend; as a horseman, a swordsman, a Christian,
      Was he known, far and wide.

This digression pray pardon. 'Twas there that he raised us together—
      Old Beau there and me.
Though Beau was a nigger, and I was the son of his owner,
      Not a tittle cared we;
We were simply two boys—we were friends—we were constant companions
      In work or on spree.

Well, a cousin of mine, James Tottett, from Washington city,
      Came over one year
To pay me a visit—a priggish young blue-blood and churlish,
      With an arrogant sneer
For our "primitive" customs, and boasting his wondrous achievements
      In tobacco and beer.

From the first, Beau conceived a dislike to James, "the town-tackey,"
      Which he sought not to hide;
While James was accustomed to make him the butt of his banter,
      And frequently tried
To goad him by taunts to a quarrel, to which the young darkey
      Very seldom replied.

One Sabbath we went, with a lot of the neighboring youngsters—
  Inclusive of Beau
And of James—to the river near by, our ultimate purpose
  A-swimming to go.
Walking thither James ridiculed Beau more severely than usual
  (If he could have done so.)

Now Beau was a wondrous musician on whistles and fiddles,
  Which he made with his knife,
And the Christmas preceding my father had brought him from
  Richmond
  A marvellous fife,
To perform upon which, to his friends' and his own delectation,
  Was the pride of his life.

And upon this occasion his fife, from his pocket projecting,
  In view of us all,
Was snatched at by James. Then they clinched. In the tussle
  ensuing,
  Beau was rather too small :
James gave him a drubbing, and then put the fife in *his* pocket,
  Thus concluding the brawl.

We continued our journey until we arrived at the river,
  Our prime destination ;
Our ablutions performed, our habiliments donned, 'twas suggested
  That, for more recreation,
We proceed up the stream to the "Door of the Devil" which
  motion
  Received approbation.

This Door of the Devil was then a notorious feature
  In the river hard by,
Where the water dashed swirling beneath the steep bank exca-
  vated,
  With a sough and a sigh ;
And never again had aught swallowed down by its current
  Been perceived by man's eye.

Arrived, we were gazing with wonder down at the white waters,
        And with some superstition,
When, attempting to cast an unwieldy projectile into them,
        James lost his position—
Falling in—in a trice sucked from sight—while we stood stark as
    statues,
        In our helpless condition.

Great God! Not an atom of hope! Yet some one cried "Mur-
    der!"
        In response to which call
Came a number of parties—among them were Beau and my father,
        (Beau after the brawl
Having sulked in the rear)—and despair and a sickening horror
        Filled the faces of all.

No hope; for the Door of the Devil never yields up its victims,
        And none is so rash
As to forfeit his life in a futile endeavor to rescue,
        Nor—Hold!—like a flash,
A figure darts through us—leaps over the bank—in an instant
        Disappears with a splash.

It was Beau! There's a breeze of a murmur, and then a dead
    silence;
        He can ne'er reappear:
This we know, even though he is one of the finest of divers
        To be found far or near.
Thus we wait a full minute—another—*two heads above water!*
        And from us a hoarse cheer.

There's a fearful suspense—a grand struggle—and Beau, with his
    burden,
        At last is ashore;
And the men rear him, dripping and bleeding, aloft on their
    shoulders,
        With a thunderous roar.
And my father for once is profane, as he swears, "By Jehovah!
        He is FREE, evermore!"

When James had recovered, he walked up to Beau, and he
    thanked him,
       . And assured him James Tottett
Was his friend from that forth, and he offered his hand, but Beau
    scorned it,
       And muttered, " Dod rot it !
Do you think it war YOU I war after ? " (his hand on his pocket)—
       " 'Twar my *fife* and I got it ! "

T. H. Robertson.

BILL MASON'S BRIDE.

HALF an hour till train time, sir,
    An' a fearful dark night, too;
Take a look at the switch-lights, Tom,
    Fetch in a stick when you're through.
"On time ? " well, yes, I guess so—
    Left the last station all right ;
She'll come round the curve a flyin'—
    Bill Mason comes up to-night.

You know Bill ? No ! he's engineer ;
    Been on the road all his life :
I'll never forget the mornin'
    He married his chunk of a wife.
'Twas the summer the mill hands struck—
    Jest off work, every one ;
They kicked up a row in the village,
    And killed old Donovan's son.

Bill hedn't been married more'n an hour,
    Up comes a message from Kress,
Orderin' Bill to go up there
    And bring down the night express.

He left his gal in a hurry
    And went up on number one,
Thinkin' of nothin' but Mary
    And the train he had to run.

And Mary sat by the window
    To wait for the night express ;
An', sir, if she hadn't ha' done so,
    She'd been a widow, I guess.
For it must ha' been nigh midnight
    When them mill hands left the Ridge ;
They come down—the drunken devils !—
    Tore up a rail from the bridge.
But Mary heard 'em a workin',
    And guessed there was somethin' wrong—
And in less than fifteen minutes
    Bill's train it would be along !

She couldn't ha' come here to tell *us*,
    A mile—it wouldn't ha' done ;
So she jest grabbed up a lantern
    And made for the bridge alone.
Then down came the night express, sir,
    And Bill was makin' her climb !
But Mary held the lantern,
    A swingin' it all the time.

Well, by Jove ! Bill saw the signal,
    And he stopped the night express,
And he found his Mary cryin'
    On the track, in her weddin' dress ;
Cryin' an' laughin' for joy, sir,
    An' holdin' on to the light—
Hallo ! here's the train ! good-by, sir,
    Bill Mason's on time to-night !

Chiquita.

THE SPANISH ARMADA.

COME all ye who list to hear our noble England's praise,
I'll tell you the thrice famous deeds she wrought in ancient days ;
When that great fleet invincible, against her bore in vain,
The richest spoils of Mexico, the stoutest hearts of Spain.
'Twas about the lovely close of a warm summer's day,
There came a gallant merchant ship, full sail to Plymouth Bay ;
Her crew had seen Castile's black fleet, beyond Aurigny's Isle,
At earliest twilight on the wave lie heaving many a mile.
At sunrise, she escaped their van by God's especial grace,
But the tall Pinta, till the noon, had kept her close in chase ;
Forthwith a guard at every gun was placed along the wall,
The beacon blazed upon the roof of Edgecomb's lofty hall ;
And many a fishing bark put out to pry along the coast,
And with loose rein and bloody spur rode inland many a post,
With his white hair unbonnetted, the stout old sheriff comes,
Behind him march the halberdiers, before him sound the drums.
His yeomen round the Market-cross make clear an ample space,
For it behooves him to set up the standard of Her Grace.
And haughtily the trumpet peals, and gayly dance the bells,
As slow upon the laboring wind the royal blazon swells.
Look ! how the Lion of the Sea lifts up his ancient crown,
And underneath his deadly paw treads the gay *lilies* down ;
So stalked he when he turned to flight, on that famed Picard,
    field,
Bohemia's plume, Genoa's bow, and Cæsar's eagle shield ;
So glared he when, at Agincourt in wrath, he turned to bay,
And crushed and torn, beneath his claws, the princely hunters lay.
Ho ! strike the flagstaff deep, Sir Knight. Ho ! scatter flowers
    fair maids
Ho ! gunners, fire a loud salute. Ho ! gallants, draw your
    blades.
The sun, shine on her joyously,—ye breezes, waft her wide,
Our glorious *Semper eadem*, the banner of our pride,

The freshening breeze of eve unfurled the banner's massy fold,
The parting gleam of sunshine kissed the haughty scroll of gold.
Night sank upon the dusky beach, and on the purple sea,
Such night in England ne'er had been, and ne'er again shall be.
From Eddystone to Berwick bound, from Lynn to Milford Bay,
The time of slumber was as bright and busy as the day;
For swift to east, and swift to west the ghastly war-flame spread,
High on St. Michael's Mount it shone, it shone on Beechy Head.
Far on the deep the Spaniards saw along each Southern shire,
Cape beyond cape, in endless range, those twinkling points of fire.
The fisher left his skiff to rock on Tamar's glittering waves,
The rugged poured to war from Mendip's sunless caves.
O'er Longleat's towers, o'er Cranbourne's oaks the fiery heralds
    flew;
They roused the Shepherds of Stonehenge, the rangers of Beau-
    lieu.
Right sharp and quick the bells rang out all night from Bristol
    town,
And ere the day three hundred horse had met on Clifton-Down.
The sentinel in Whitehall gate looked forth into the night,
And saw o'erhanging Richmond hill a streak of blood-red light.
Then bugle note, and cannon roar, the deathlike stillness broke,
And with one start, and with one cry, the royal city woke!
At once on all her stately gates arose the answering fires,
At once the wild alarum clashed from all her reeling spires.
From all the batteries of the Tower pealed loud the voice of fear,
And all the thousand masts of Thames sent back a louder cheer;
And from the farthest wards was heard the rush of hurrying feet,
Broad streams of flags and pikes dashed down each roaring street.
And broader still became the blaze, and louder still the din,
As fast from every village round, the horse came spurring in,
And eastward straight from wild Blackheath the warlike errand
    went,
And roused in many an ancient hall the gallant Squires of Kent;
Southward of Surrey's pleasant hills, flew those bright couriers
    forth,
High on bleak Hampstead's swarthy moor they started from the
    north;

And on, and on, without a pause, untired they bounded still,—
All night from tower to tower they sprang, they sprang from hill
   to hill,
Till the proud peak unfurled the flag o'er Darwin's rocky dales,
Till like volcanoes flared to heaven, the stormy hills of Wales,
Till twelve fair counties saw the blaze on Malvern's lonely hight,
Till streamed in crimson on the wind the Wrekin's crest of light;
Till broad and fierce the star came forth on Ely's stately fane
And tower and hamlet rose in arms o'er all the boundless plain;
Till Belvoir's lordly terraces the sign to Lincoln sent,
And Lincoln sped the message on o'er the wide vale of Trent.
Till Skiddaw saw the fire that burned on Gaunt's embattled pile,
And the red glare on Skiddaw roused the Burghers of Carlisle.

Lord Macaulay.

HENRY OF NAVARRE BEFORE PARIS.

From Harper's Magazine.

SIXTEENTH CENTURY.

DOWN upon the 'leaguered town
With forty thousand men he rode:
The fields were bare, the meadows brown,
   The starving cattle faintly lowed.

But conquering hero, he rode down—
As if to hawk and bells he rode—
While fields were bare and meadows brown
   And starving cattle faintly lowed.

And just without the 'leaguered town
They pitched their tents along the road,
Or in the fields and meadows brown,
   Where starving cattle faintly lowed.

6

Day after day they stormed the town;
Day after day he laughing rode
Across the fields and meadows brown,
    Where starving cattle faintly lowed.

One day from out the 'leaguered town
There faltered forth along the road,
And by the fields and meadows brown,
    Where starving cattle faintly lowed,

A wretched throng. The 'leaguered town
Had cast aside its useless load,
And by the fields and meadows brown,
    Where starving cattle faintly lowed,

They faltered up, they faltered down,
Half dazed with fear, along the road.
Then, by the fields and meadows brown,
    Where starving cattle faintly lowed.

The hero who had stormed the town
Day after day, and careless rode
Day after day by meadows brown,
    Where starving cattle faintly lowed,

With swift, sharp strokes came riding down
Along the white and dusty road,
Unheeding still the meadows brown,
    The starving cattle as they lowed.

His face was set beneath a frown;
His laughing eyes, that had bestowed
No glance upon the meadows brown,
    Where starving cattle faintly lowed.

Now fierce, yet soft, looked shining down
Upon the groups that thronged the road,
Blind to the meadows bare and brown,
    Deaf to the cattle as they lowed.

His great heart suddenly bore down
The conqueror's pride, and back he rode,
Past all the fields and meadows brown,
      Where starving cattle faintly lowed.

He fed the people of the town—
These famished groups that thronged the road
And through the fields and meadows brown
      He called the cattle as they lowed,

And fed them all. Then from the town
He turned away and lightly rode
Past all the fields and meadows brown,
      With face that shone and eyes that glowed.

" *Vive Dieu!* " he cried, " I'll take no town
By famine's scourge : a fairer road
Must Henry of Navarre ride down
      To find his triumphs well bestowed."
                    Nora Perry.

THE DEFENCE OF LUCKNOW.

BANNER of England, not for a season, O banner of Britain, hast
    thou
Floated in conquering battle or flapt to the battle-cry !
Never with mightier glory than when we had rear'd thee on high
Flying at top of the roofs in the ghastly siege of Lucknow—
Shot thro' the staff or the halyard, but ever we raised thee anew,
And ever upon the topmost roof our banner of England blew.

Frail were the works that defended the hold that we held with
    our lives—
Women and children among us, God help them, our children and
    wives !
Hold it we might—and for fifteen days or for twenty at most.
" Never surrender, I charge you, but every man die at his post!"

Voice of the dead whom we loved, our Lawrence, the best of the
brave :
Cold were his brows when we kiss'd him—we laid him that night
in his grave.
" Every man die at his post ! " and there hail'd on our houses and
halls
Death from their rifle-bullets, and death from their cannon-balls,
Death in our innermost chamber, and death at our slight barri-
cade,
Death while we stood with the musket, and death while we
stoopt to the spade,
Death to the dying, and wounds to the wounded, for often there
fell
Striking the hospital wall, crashing thro' it, their shot and their
shell,
Death—for their spies were among us, their marksmen were told
of our best,
So that the brute bullet broke thro' the brain that could think for
the rest ;
Bullets would sing by our foreheads, and bullets would rain at our
feet—
Fire from ten thousand at once of the rebels that girdled us
round—
Death at the glimpse of a finger from over the breadth of a street,
Death from the heights of the mosque and the palace, and death
in the ground !
Mine ? yes, a mine ! Countermine ! down, down ! and creep thro'
the hole !
Keep the revolver in hand ! You can hear him—the murderous
mole.
Quiet, ah ! quiet—wait till the point of the pickaxe be thro' !
Click with the pick, coming nearer and nearer again than before—
Now let it speak, and you fire, and the dark pioneer is no more ;
And ever upon the topmost roof our banner of England blew.

Ay, but the foe sprung his mine many times, and it chanced on a
day
Soon as the blast of that underground thunderclap echo'd away,

Dark thro' the smoke and the sulphur like so many fiends in their
    hell—
Cannon-shot, musket-shot, volley on volley, and yell upon yell—
Fiercely on all the defences our myriad enemy fell.
What have they done? where is it? Out yonder. Guard the
    Redan!
Storm at the Water-gate! Storm at the Bailey-gate! storm, and
    it ran
Surging and swaying all round us, as ocean on every side
Plunges and heaves at a bank that is daily drown'd by the tide—
So many thousands that if they be bold enough, who shall escape?
Kill or be kill'd, live or die, they shall know we are soldiers and
    men!
Ready! take aim at their leaders—their masses are gapp'd with
    our grape—
Backward they reel like the wave, like the wave flinging forward
    again,
Flying and foil'd at the last by the handful they could not subdue;
And ever upon the topmost roof our banner of England blew.

Handful of men as we were, we were English in heart and in limb,
Strong with the strength of the race to command, to obey, to en-
    dure,
Each of us fought as if hope for the garrison hung but on him;
Still—could we watch at all points? we were every day fewer and
    fewer.
There was a whisper among us, but only a whisper that past;
"Children and wives—if the tigers leap into the fold unawares—
Every man die at his post—and the foe may outlive us at last—
Better to fall by the hands that they love, than to fall into theirs!"
Roar upon roar in a moment two mines by the enemy sprung
Clove into perilous chasms our walls and our poor palisades.
Rifleman, true is your heart, but be sure that your hand be as true!
Sharp is the fire of assault, better aim'd are your flank fusillades—
Twice do we hurl them to earth from the ladders to which they
    had clung,
Twice from the ditch where they shelter we drive them with hand-
    grenades:
And ever upon the topmost roof our banner of England blew.

Then on another wild morning another wild earthquake out-tore
Clean from our lines of defence ten or twelve good paces or more.
Rifleman, high on the roof, hidden there from the light of the
    sun—
One has leapt up on the breach, crying out: " Follow me, follow
    me!"—
Mark him—he falls! then another, and *him* too, and down goes
    he.
Had they been bold enough then, who can tell but the traitors had
    won ?
Boardings and rafters and doors—an embrasure! make way for
    the gun !
Now double-charge it with grape! It is charged and we fire, and
    they run.
Praise to our Indian brothers, and let the dark face have his due !
Thanks to the kindly dark faces who fought with us, faithful and
    few,
Fought with the bravest among us, and drove them, and smote
    them, and slew,
That ever upon the topmost roof our banner in India blew.

Men will forget what we suffer and not what we do. We can
    fight ;
But to be soldier all day and be sentinel all through the night—
Ever the mine and assault, our sallies, their lying alarms,
Bugles and drums in the darkness, and shoutings and soundings
    to arms,
Ever the labor of fifty that had to be done by five,
Ever the marvel among us that one should be left alive,
Ever the day with its traitorous death from the loop-holes around,
Ever the night with its coffinless corpse to be laid in the ground,
Heat like the mouth of a hell, or a deluge of cataract skies,
Stench of old offal decaying, and infinite torment of flies,
Thoughts of the breezes of May blowing over an English field,
Cholera, scurvy, and fever, the wound that *would* not be healed,
Lopping away of the limb by the pitiful-pitiless knife—
Torture and trouble in vain—for it never could save us a life,
Valor of delicate women who tended the hospital bed,
Horror of women in travail among the dying and dead,

Grief for our perishing children, and never a moment for grief,
Toil and ineffable weariness, faltering hopes of relief,
Havelock baffled, or beaten, or butchered for all that we knew—
Then day and night, day and night, coming down on the still-shat-
tered walls
Millions of musket-bullets, and thousands of cannon-balls—
But ever upon the topmost roof our banner of England blew.

Hark cannonade, fusillade! is it true what was told by the scout?
Outram and Havelock breaking their way through the fell muti-
neers !
Surely the pibroch of Europe is ringing again in our ears !
All on a sudden the garrison utter a jubilant shout,
Havelock's glorious Highlanders answer with conquering cheers,
Forth from their holes and their hidings our women and children
come out,
Blessing the wholesome white faces of Havelock's good fusileers,
Kissing the war-hardened hand of the Highlander wet with their
tears!
Dance to the pibroch!—saved! we are saved!—is it you? is it
you?
Saved by the valor of Havelock, saved by the blessing of Heaven !
"Hold it for fifteen days !" we have held it for eighty-seven !
And ever aloft on the palace roof the old banner of England
blew.

Alfred Tennyson.

EXECUTION OF QUEEN MARY.

THE Queen arrived in the hall of death. Pale but
unflinching she contemplated the dismal preparations.
There lay the block and the axe. There stood the executioner and his assistant. All were clothed in
mourning. On the floor was scattered the sawdust

which was to soak her blood, and in a dark corner lay the bier. It was nine o'clock when the Queen appeared in the funereal hall. Fletcher, Dean of Peterborough, and certain privileged persons, to the number of more than two hundred, were assembled. The hall was hung with black cloth; the scaffold, which was el⁻evated about two feet and a half above the ground, was covered with black frieze of Lancaster; the arm-chair in which Mary was to sit, the footstool on which she was to kneel, the block on which her head was to be laid, were covered with black velvet.

The Queen was clothed in mourning like the hall and as the ensign of punishment. Her black velvet robe, with its high collar and hanging sleeves, was bordered with ermine. Her mantle, lined with marten sable, was of satin, with pearl buttons and a long train. A chain of sweet-smelling beads, to which was attached a scapulary, and beneath that a golden cross, fell upon her bosom. Two rosaries were suspended to her girdle, and a long veil of white lace, which in some measure softened this costume of a widow and of a condemned criminal, was thrown around her.

Arrived on the scaffold, Mary seated herself in the chair provided for her, with her face toward the spectators. The Dean of Peterborough, in ecclesiastical costume, sat on the right of the Queen, with a black velvet footstool before him. The Earls of Kent and Shrewsbury were seated, like him, on the right, but upon larger chairs. On the other side of the Queen stood the Sheriff, Andrews, with white wand. In front of Mary were seen the executioner and his assistant, distinguishable by their vestments of black velvet with red crape round the left arm.   Behind the Queen's chair, ranged by the wall, wept her attendants and maidens.

In the body of the hall, the nobles and citizens from the neighboring counties were guarded by musketeers. Beyond the balustrade was the bar of the tribunal. The sentence was read; the Queen protested against *it* in the name of royalty and of innocence, but accepted death for the sake of the faith.   She then knelt before the block and the executioner proceeded to remove her veil.   She repelled him by a gesture, and turning toward the Earls with a blush on her forehead, "I am not accustomed," she said, " to be undressed before so numerous a company, and by the hands of such grooms of the chamber."

She then called Jane Kennedy and Elizabeth Curle, who took off her mantle, her veil, her chains, cross, and scapulary.   On their touching her robe, the Queen told them to unloosen the corsage and fold down the ermine collar, so as to leave her neck bare for the axe. Her maidens weepingly yielded her these last services. Melvil and the three other attendants wept and lamented, and Mary placed her finger on her lips to signify that they should be silent.   She then arranged the handkerchief embroidered with thistles of gold with which her eyes had been covered by Jane Kennedy.

Thrice she kissed the crucifix, each time repeating, "Lord, into Thy hands I commend my spirit."   She knelt anew and leant her head on that block which was already scored with deep marks, and in this solemn attitude she again recited some verses from the Psalms. The executioner interrupted her at the third verse by a blow of the axe, but its trembling stroke only grazed

her neck ; she groaned slightly, and the second blow
separated the head from the body.—*Lamartine.*

CURFEW MUST NOT RING TO-NIGHT.

ENGLAND'S sun was slowly setting o'er the hills so far away,
Filling all the land with beauty at the close of one sad day ;
And the last rays kiss'd the forehead of a man and maiden fair,
He with step so slow and weakened, she with sunny floating
    hair ;
He with sad bowed head, and thoughtful, she with lips so cold
    and white,
Struggling to keep back the murmur, " Curfew must not ring to-
    night."
" Sexton," Bessie's white lips faltered, pointing to the prison
    old,
With its walls so dark and gloomy—walls so dark and damp and
    cold—
" I've a lover in that prison, doomed this very night to die
At the ringing of the Curfew, and no earthly help is nigh.
Cromwell will not come till sunset," and her face grew strangely
    white,
As she spoke in husky whispers, " Curfew must not ring to-
    night."
" Bessie," calmly spoke the sexton—every word pierced her
    young heart
Like a thousand gleaming arrows, like a deadly-poisoned dart—
" Long, long years I've rung the Curfew from that gloomy shad-
    owed tower ;
Every evening, just at sunset, it has told the twilight hour ;
I have done my duty ever, tried to do it just and right,
Now I'm old I will not miss it ; girl, the Curfew rings to-night !"
Wild her eyes and pale her features, stern and white her thought
    ful brow,
And within her heart's deep centre, Bessie made a solemn vow ;

She had listened while the judges read, without a tear or sigh,
" At the ringing of the Curfew—Basil Underwood *must die*."
And her breath came fast and faster, and her eyes grew large and bright—
One low murmur, scarcely spoken—" Curfew *must not* ring to-night ! "
She with light step bounded forward, sprang within the old church door,
Left the old man coming slowly paths he'd trod so oft before ;
Not one moment paused the maiden, but with cheek and brow aglow,
Staggered up the gloomy tower, where the bell swung to and fro ;
Then she climbed the slimy ladder, dark, without one ray of light,
Upward still, her pale lips saying: " Curfew shall not ring to-night."
She has reached the topmost ladder, o'er her hangs the great dark bell ;
And the awful gloom beneath her, like the pathway down to hell ;
See, the ponderous tongue is swinging, 'tis the hour of Curfew now,
And the sight has chilled her bosom, stopped her breath and . paled her brow.
Shall she let it ring ? No, never ! her eyes flash with sudden light,
As she springs and grasps it firmly—" Curfew shall not ring to-night ! "
Out she swung, far out, the city seemed a tiny speck below ;
There, 'twixt heaven and earth suspended, as the bell swung to and fro ;
And the half-deaf sexton ringing (years he had not heard the bell),
And he thought the twilight Curfew rang young Basil's funeral knell ;
Still the maiden clinging firmly, cheek and brow so pale and white,
Stilled her frightened heart's wild beating—" *Curfew shall not ring to-night.*"

It was o'er —the bell ceased swaying, and the maiden stepped
    once more
Firmly on the damp old ladder, where for hundred years before
Human foot had not been planted; and what she this night had
    done
Should be told in long years after—as the rays of setting sun
Light the sky with mellow beauty, aged sires with heads of white
Tell their children why the Curfew did not ring that one sad
    night.
O'er the distant hills came Cromwell; Bessie saw him, and her
    brow,
Lately white with sickening terror, glows with sudden beauty
    now;
At his feet she told her story, showed her hands all bruised and
    torn;
And her sweet young face so haggard, with a look so sad and
    worn,
Touched his heart with sudden pity—lit his eyes with misty
    light;
"Go, your lover lives!" cried Cromwell; "Curfew shall not
    ring to-night."

Anon.

HOW HE SAVED ST. MICHAEL'S.

'TWAS long ago—ere ever the signal gun
That blazed before Fort Sumter had wakened the North as one;
Long ere the wondrous pillar of battle-cloud and fire
Had marked where the unchained millions marched on to their
    heart's desire.
On roofs and glittering turrets, that night, as the sun went down,
The mellow glow of the twilight shone like a jewelled crown,
And, bathed in the living glory, as the people lifted their eyes,
They saw the pride of the city, the spire of St. Michael's, rise

High over the lesser steeples, tipped with a golden ball,
That hung like a radiant planet caught in its earthward fall;

First glimpse of home to the sailor who made the harbor round,
And last slow-fading vision dear to the outward bound.
The gently-gathering shadows shut out the waning light;
The children prayed at their bedsides as they were wont each
night;
The noise of buyer and seller from the busy mart was gone,
And in dreams of a peaceful morrow the city slumbered on.

But another light than sunrise aroused the sleeping street,
For a cry was heard at midnight, and the rush of trampling feet;
Men stared in each other's faces, thro' mingled fire and smoke,
While the frantic bells went clashing clamorous, stroke on
stroke.
By the glare of her blazing roof-tree the houseless mother fled,
With the babe she pressed to her bosom shrieking in nameless
dread;
While the fire-king's wild battalions scaled wall and capstone
high,
And planted their glaring banners against an inky sky.
From the death that raged behind them, and the crush of ruin
loud,
To the great square of the city, were driven the surging crowd,
Where yet firm in all the tumult, unscathed by the fiery flood,
With its heavenward pointing finger the church of St. Michael's
stood.

But e'en as they gazed upon it there rose a sudden wail,
A cry of horror blended with the roaring of the gale,
On whose scorching wings updriven, a single flaming brand,
Aloft on the towering steeple clung like a bloody hand.
"Will it fade?" the whisper trembled from a thousand whiten-
ing lips;
Far out on the lurid harbor they watched it from the ships.
A baleful gleam, that brighter and ever brighter shone,
Like a flickering, trembling will-o'-the-wisp to a steady beacon
grown.
"Uncounted gold shall be given to the man whose brave right
hand,
For the love of the perilled city, plucks down yon burning brand!"

So cried the Mayor of Charleston, that all the people heard,
But they looked each one at his fellow, and no man spoke a word.
Who is it leans from the belfry, with face upturned to the sky—
Clings to a column and measures the dizzy spire with his eye?
Will he dare it, the hero undaunted, that terrible, sickening
    height,
Or will the hot blood of his courage freeze in his veins at the
    sight?
But see! he has stepped on the railing, he climbs with his feet
    and his hands,
And firm on a narrow projection, with the belfry beneath him, he
    stands!
Now once, and once only, they cheer him—a single tempestuous
    breath,
And there falls on the multitude gazing a hush like the stillness
    of death.
Slow, steadily mounting, unheeding aught save the goal of the fire,
Still higher and higher, an atom, he moves on the face of the
    spire;
He stops! Will he fall? Lo! for answer, a gleam like a me-
    teor's track,
And, hurled on the stones of the pavement, the red brand lies
    shattered and black!
Once more the shouts of the people have rent the quivering air;
At the church door mayor and council wait with their feet on the
    stair,
And the eager throng behind them press for a touch of his
    hand—
The unknown savior whose daring could compass a deed so grand.

But why does a sudden tremor seize on them as they gaze?
And what meaneth that stifled murmur of wonder and amaze?
He stood in the gate of the temple he had perilled his life to save,
And the face of the unknown hero was the sable face of a slave!
With folded arms he was speaking in tones that were clear, not
    loud,
And his eyes, ablaze in their sockets, burnt into the eyes of the
    crowd.

" Ye may keep your gold, I scorn it! but answer me, ye who can,
If the deed I have done before you be not the deed of a *man ?* "

He stepped but a short space backward, and from all the women
and men
There were only sobs for answer, and the mayor called for a pen,
And the great seal of the city, that he might read who ran,
And the slave who saved St. Michael's went out from its door a
man.

Mary A. P. Stansbury.

BETH GELERT.

THE spearman heard the bugle sound, and cheerly smiled the
morn,
And many a brach and many a hound attend Llewellyn's horn;
And still he blew a louder blast, and gave a louder cheer:
" Come, Gelert! why art thou the last Llewellyn's horn to hear?
Oh, where does faithful Gelert roam? the flower of all his race!
So true, so brave! a lamb at home—a lion in the chase!"

'Twas only at Llewellyn's board the faithful Gelert fed;
He watched, he served, he cheered his lord, and sentinell'd his bed.
In sooth, he was a peerless hound, the gift of royal John—
But now no Gelert could be found, and all the chase rode on.
And now, as over rocks and dells the gallant chidings rise,
All Snowdon's craggy chaos yells with many mingled cries.
That day Llewellyn little loved the chase of hart or hare,
And scant and small the booty proved—for Gelert was not there.
Unpleased, Llewellyn homeward hied; when, near the portal seat,
His truant Gelert he espied, bounding his lord to greet.
But when he gained the castle door, aghast the chieftain stood;
The hound was smeared with gouts of gore:—his lips and fangs
ran blood!
Llewellyn gazed with wild surprise, unused such looks to meet;
His favorite checked his joyful guise, and crouched, and licked
his feet.

Onward in haste Llewellyn passed—and on went Gelert too;
And still, where'er his eyes were cast, fresh blood-gouts shocked
    his view !
O'erturned his infant's bed he found! the blood-stained covert
    rent ;
And all around the walls and ground with recent blood besprent!
He called his child—no voice replied! he searched with terror
    wild :
Blood! blood! he found on every side, but nowhere found the
    child !
"Hell-hound! by thee my child's devoured!" the frantic father
    cried,
And to the hilt his vengeful sword he plunged in Gelert's side!—
His suppliant as to earth he fell no pity could impart;
But still his Gelert's dying yell passed heavy o'er his heart.

Aroused by Gelert's dying yell, some slumberer wakened nigh;
What words the parent's joy can tell, to hear his infant cry!
Concealed beneath a mangled heap his hurried search had missed,
All glowing from his rosy sleep his cherub boy he kissed!
Nor scratch had he, nor harm, nor dread—but the same couch be-
    neath
Lay a great wolf, all torn and dead—tremendous still in death !

Ah! what was then Llewellyn's pain! for now the truth was clear
The gallant hound the wolf had slain, to save Llewellyn's heir.
Vain, vain was all Llewellyn's woe : "Best of thy kind, adieu !
The frantic deed which laid thee low this heart shall ever rue !"
And now a gallant tomb they raise, with costly sculpture decked ;
And marbles, storied with his praise, poor Gelert's bones protect.
Here never could the spearman pass, or forester, unmoved,
Here oft the tear besprinkled grass Llewellyn's sorrow proved.
And here he hung his horn and spear; and oft, as evening fell,
In fancy's piercing sounds would hear poor Gelert's dying yell !

                            W. L. Spencer.

THE LITTLE HERO.

Now, lads, a short yarn I'll just spin you,
    As happened on our very last run—
'Bout a boy as a man's soul had in him,
    Or else I'm a son of a gun.

From Liverpool port out three days, lads;
    The good ship floating over the deep;
The skies bright with sunshine above us;
    The waters beneath us asleep.

Not a bad-tempered lubber among us;
    A jollier crew never sailed,
'Cept the first mate, a bit of a savage,
    But good seaman as ever was hailed.

Regulation, good order, his motto;
    Strong as iron, steady as quick;
With a couple of bushy black eyebrows,
    And eyes fierce as those of Old Nick.

One day he comes up from below,
    A-graspin' a lad by the arm—
A poor little ragged young urchin
    As had ought to bin home to his marm.

An' the mate asks the boy, pretty roughly,
    How he dared for to be stowed away,
A-cheatin' the owners and captain,
    Sailin', eatin', and all without pay.

The lad had a face bright and sunny,
    An' a pair of blue eyes like a girl's,
An' looks up at the scowlin' first mate, lads,
    An' shakes back his long, shining curls.

7

An' says he, in a voice dear and pretty,
    " My step-father brought me aboard,
And hid me away down the stairs there;
    For to keep me he couldn't afford.

" And he told me the big ship would take me
    To Halifax town—oh, so far !
And he said, ' Now the Lord is your father,
    Who lives where the good angels are.' "

" It's a lie," says the mate ; " not your father,
    But some of these big skulkers aboard;
Some milk-hearted, soft-headed sailor.
    Speak up, tell the truth, d'ye hear ? "

" 'Twarn't us," growled the tars as stood round 'em.
    " What's your age ? " says one of the brine.
" And your name ? " says another old salt fish.
    Says the small chap, " I'm Frank, just turned nine."

"Oh, my eyes ! " says another bronzed seaman
    To the mate, who seemed staggered hisself,
" Let him go free to old Novy Scoshy,
    And I'll work out his passage myself."

" Belay ! " says the mate : "shut your mouth, man !
    I'll sail this 'ere craft, bet your life,
An' I'll fit the lie onto you somehow,
    As square as a fork fits a knife."

Then a-knitting his black brows with anger,
    He tumbled the poor slip below;
An', says he, " P'r'aps to-morrow'll change you ;
    If it don't, back to England you go."

I took him some dinner, be sure, mates,
    Just think, only nine years of age !
An' next day, just as six bells tolled,
    The mate brings him up from his cage.

An' he plants him before us amidships,
  His eyes like two coals all a-light;
An' he says, through his teeth, mad with passion,
  An' his hand lifted ready to smite.

" Tell the truth, lad, and then I'll forgive you ;
  But the truth I will have.   Speak it out.
It wasn't your father as brought you,
  But some of these men hereabout."

Then that pair o' blue eyes, bright and winning,
  Clear and shining with innocent youth,
Looks up at the mate's bushy eyebrows ;
  An', says he, " Sir, I've told you the truth."

'Twarn't no use: the mate didn't believe him,
  Though every man else did, aboard,
With rough hand by the collar he seized him,
  And cried, " You shall hang, by the Lord ! "

An' he snatched his watch out of his pocket,
  Just as if he'd been drawin' a knife.
" If in ten minutes more you don't speak, lad
  There's the rope, and good-by to your life."

There ! you never see such a sight, mates,
  As that boy with his bright, pretty face—
Proud, though, and steady with courage,
  Never thinking of asking for grace.

Eight minutes went by all in silence.
  Says the mate then, " Speak, lad : say your say."
His eyes slowly filling with tear-drops,
  He faltering says, " May I pray ? "

I'm a rough and hard old tarpa'lin
  As any " blue-jacket " afloat ;
But the salt water springs to my eyes, lads,
  And I felt my heart rise in my throat.

The mate kind o' trembled an' shivered,
  And nodded his head in reply;
And his cheek went all white of a sudden,
  And the hot light was quenched in his eye.

Tho' he stood like a figure of marble,
  With his watch tightly grasped in his hand,
And the passengers all still around him :
  Ne'er the like was on sea or on land.

An' the little chap kneels on the deck there,
  An' his hands he clasps over his breast,
As he must ha' done often at home, lads,
  At night-time, when going to rest.

And soft come the first words, " Our Father,"
  Low and soft from the dear baby-lip;
But, low as they were, heard like trumpet .
  By each true man aboard of that ship.

Ev'ry bit of that prayer, mates, he goes through,
  To, " Forever and ever.   Amen."
And for all the bright gold of the Indies
  I wouldn't ha' heard it again.

And, says he, when he finished, uprising
  An' lifting his blue eyes above,
" Dear Lord Jesus, oh, take me to Heaven,
  Back again to my own mother's love !"

For a minute or two, like a magic,
  We stood every man like the dead.
Then back to the mate's face comes running
  The life-blood again, warm and red.

Off his feet was that lad sudden lifted,
  And clasped to the mate's rugged breast;
And his husky voice muttered " God bless you !"
  As his lips to his forehead he pressed.

If the ship hadn't been a good sailer,
  And gone by herself right along,
All had gone to Old Davy; for all, lads,
  Was gathered 'round in that throng.

Like a man, says the mate, " God forgive me,
  That ever I used you so hard.
It's myself as had ought to be strung up,
  Taut and sure, to that ugly old yard."

" You believe me, then? " said the youngster.
  " Believe you! " He kissed him once more.
" You'd have laid down your life for the truth, lad?
  Believe you! From now, evermore! "

An' p'r'aps, mates, he wasn't thought much on
  All that day and the rest of the trip;
P'r'aps, he paid, after all, for his passage;
  P'r'aps he wasn't the pet of the ship!

An' if that little chap ain't a model
  For all, young or old, short or tall,
And if that ain't the stuff to make men of,
  Old Ben, he knows naught after all.

Matthison.

THE POLISH BOY.

WHENCE come those shrieks so wild and shrill,
  That cut, like blades of steel, the air,
Causing the creeping blood to chill
  With the sharp cadence of despair?

Again they come, as if a heart
  Were cleft in twain by one quick blow,
And every string had voice apart
  To utter its peculiar woe.

Whence came they? from yon temple where
An altar, raised for private prayer,
Now forms the warrior's marble bed
Who Warsaw's gallant armies led.

The dim funereal tapers throw
A holy lustre o'er his brow,
And burnish with their rays of light
The mass of curls that gather bright
Above the haughty brow and eye
Of a young boy that's kneeling by.

What hand is that, whose icy press
   Clings to the dead with death's own grasp,
But meets no answering caress?
   No thrilling fingers seek its clasp?
It is the hand of her whose cry
   Rang wildly, late, upon the air,
When the dead warrior met her eye
   Outstretched upon the altar there.

With pallid lip and stony brow
She murmurs forth her anguish now.
But hark! the tramp of heavy feet
Is heard along the bloody street;
Nearer and nearer yet they come,
With clanking arms and noiseless drum.
Now whispered curses, low and deep,
Around the holy temple creep;
The gate is burst; a ruffian band
Rush in and savagely demand,
With brutal voice and oath profane,
The startled boy for exile's chain.

The mother sprang with gesture wild,
And to her bosom clasped her child;
Then with pale cheek and flashing eye
Shouted with fearful energy,
" Back, ruffians, back, nor dare to tread
Too near the body of my dead;

Nor touch the living boy—I stand
Between him and your lawless band.
Take me, and bind these arms, these hands,
With Russia's heaviest iron bands,
And drag me to Siberia's wild
To perish, if 'twill save my child!"

" Peace, woman, peace! " the leader cried,
Tearing the pale boy from her side,
And in his ruffian grasp he bore
His victim to the temple door.

"One moment!" shrieked the mother; "one!
Will land or gold redeem my son?
Take heritage, take name, take all,
But leave him free from Russian thrall!
Take these!" and her white arms and hands
She stripped of rings and diamond bands,
And tore from braids of long black hair
The gems that gleamed like starlight there;
Her cross of blazing rubies last
Down at the Russian's feet she cast.
He stooped to seize the glittering store—
Upspringing from the marble floor,
The mother, with a cry of joy,
Snatched to her leaping heart the boy.
But no! the Russian's iron grasp
Again undid the mother's clasp.
Forward she fell, with one long cry
Of more than mortal agony.
But the brave child is roused at length,
   And breaking from the Russian's hold,
He stands, a giant in the strength
   Of his young spirit, fierce and bold.
Proudly he towers; his flashing eye,
   So blue, and yet so bright,
Seems kindled from the eternal sky,
   So brilliant is its light.

His curling lips and crimson cheeks
Foretell the thought before he speaks;
With a full voice of proud command
He turned upon the wondering band:
"Ye hold me not! no, no, nor can I
This hour has made the boy a man!
I knelt before my slaughtered sire,
Nor felt one throb of vengeful ire.
I wept upon his marble brow,
Yes, wept! I was a child; but now—
My noble mother, on her knee,
Hath done the work of years for me!"

He drew aside his broidered vest,
And there, like slumbering serpent's crest,
The jewelled haft of poniard bright
Glittered a moment on the sight.
"Ha! start ye back! Fool! coward! knave!
Think ye my noble father's glaive
Would drink the life-blood of a slave?
The pearls that on the handle flame
Would blush to rubies in their shame;
The blade would quiver in thy breast,
Ashamed of such ignoble rest.
No! thus I rend the tyrant's chain,
And fling him back a boy's disdain!"

A moment, and the funeral light
Flashed on the jewelled weapon bright.
Another, and his young heart's blood
Leaped to the floor, a crimson flood.
Quick to his mother's side he sprang,
And on the air his clear voice rang:
"Up, mother, up! I'm free! I'm free!
The choice was death or slavery.
Up, mother, up! Look on thy son!
His freedom is forever won;
And now he waits one holy kiss
To bear his father home in bliss—

One last embrace, one blessing—one !
To prove thou knowest, approvest thy son.
What! silent yet ? Canst thou not feel
My warm blood o'er my heart congeal ?
Speak, mother, speak ! lift up thy head !
What! silent still ? Then art thou dead ?
——Great God, I thank Thee ! Mother, I
Rejoice with thee—and thus—to die ! "
One long, deep breath, and his pale head
Lay on his mother's bosom—dead.

Ann. S. Stephens.

THE BALLAD OF RONALD CLARE.

MIDWAY up a sloping hill a grim old castle stands,
And, like a sentinel, keeps watch o'er the valley's shining lands;
Its frowning battlements are gray with the weary weight of
    years,
And of its silent chambers one is sanctified by tears.

Ah! long ago that castle's halls with merry laughter rang ;
And maiden's song, and warrior's oath, and armor's clash and
    clang.
Made glad the echoes ringing through its broad, iron-studded
    doors ;
And sunlight flecked the shadows gray along its oaken floors.

Then smiles made bright the sunny face of one long passed away,
Whose golden hair shone radiant; whose voice was blithe and
    gay
As any robin's whose red breast among the hawthorn glows
When sunlit skies and violets' breath foretell the coming rose.

The castle's lord her father was, a baron stout and bold,
With hair of gray, and brawny arm, and heart made stern and
    cold
By the hard blows of bitter frays, and forays wild and red,
When burning homes shone lurid on their owners stark and dead.

Only one joy made light his soul,—his daughter's lovely grace;
The one great vow he ne'er forswore was, " By *her* sweet bright
   face ;"
And he had marked a fate for her, as noble, high, and fair,
That he could see a crown's bright gold melt in her golden hair.

Among the knights that round his hall hung sword and lance in
   rest,
Young Ronald Clare in march or fray was always counted best:
No voice was sweeter in the camp, or had such store of song;
No hand was swifter in the fight, or e'er gave blows more strong.

And Elsie's eyes shone bright whene'er she heard his step draw
   nigh,
And sweet the smile that on her face made to his look reply ;
And even the bugle's blowing could not make Clare's heart re-
   joice
As could the rippling music of sweet Elsie's ringing voice.

Ah ! soon or late love claims the due of kisses warm and sweet,
Of looks and words, and thrills of joy, whene'er true lovers meet;
And soon or late there comes the chill of words that sting and
   pain,
And blooming cheeks and laughing eyes see their bright glory
   wane.

When daisies in the meadows bloomed, and heather clothed the
   hill,
And bird-songs all the orchard filled, and ploughmen's calls rang
   shrill,
The lovers wandered hand in hand amid the forest's shade,
And at the last by a broad stream their lingering footsteps
   strayed.

" Oh that our lives might ever run like this clear stream !" he
   said :
Then flashed a helmet on his sight; and, " Curse your caitiff
   head !"

The stern voice of the baron cried; and then, "How did you
    dare
To lift your eye so far above your state? say, Ronald Clare?"

The young man laughed: "I lift my eyes?   Methinks that you
    are mad.
Whose sword has done most work for you, of all the swords you
    had?
Whose blood has flowed the readiest to win you wealth and
    fame?
And why, I pray, is not my own as good as your old name?"

"Go to!" the baron cried, and swift his sword gleamed in his
    hand:
"There is but one name fit for her; and that, Queen of the
    Land.
So stand your ground; for now you die!"   Young Clare's laugh
    rang again:
"Not now," he said, "shall your bright sword in my blood find a
    stain.

"I go; but I shall come again.—Good-by, sweetheart!" said he;
Then sprang away.   The baron's sword rang sharply on a tree,
And quivered in the wood, as it had quivered in the head
Of Ronald Clare, had he not then quick through the forest fled.

The baron's heart was stern and sore as Elsie met his glance.
"A brave knight, truly, you have won, who fears to break a
    lance
For you!" he cried; "but, lass of mine, no more shall your fair
    face
Shine on my warriors, thus to lure them from their rightful
    place."

So in the woman's tower she was kept both night and day.
She saw afar the sunshine bright along the hilltops play;
She saw the brook go winding on among the meadows green;
And oft, adown the road, she saw an armor's shining sheen.

The hours grew to days and weeks. She saw the loom of years,
As sad and silent, rising up, and wept love's burning tears;
And then from out the valley came a bugle's stirring call,
And she could dimly hear the knights go clanking through the
hall.

And soon her maid came running in: "The king, the king, is
here!
And he would see and speak to you: so fill your face with cheer,
Your father bade me tell you come." And slowly Elsie went,
With hope and fear in surging mass within her bosom blent.

She reached the hall: a knight stood there, his armor bright with
gold,
His face safe hid beneath the bars of his dark visor's hold;
And when the baron took her hand, and led her where he stood,
Her face grew hot and brightly glowed, flushed by the rising
blood.

"My daughter, sire," the baron said: "Heaven's one best gift to
me."
The king bent low his armèd head: "A queen indeed is she,"
He murmured low; and then he cried, "I claim this lady fair!"
And, flinging up his visor, showed the face of Ronald Clare!

Anon.

A TRUE HERO.

It was in the gray of the early morning, in the season of Lent. Broad Street, from Fort Hill to State Street, was crowded with hastening worshippers, attendants on early church. Maidens, matrons, boys and men jostled and hurried on toward the churches; some with countenances sincerely sad, others with apparent attempts to appear in accord with the sombre season;

while many thoughtless and careless ones joked and chatted, laughed and scuffled along in the hurrying multitude. Suddenly a passer-by noticed tiny wreaths and puffs of smoke starting from the shingles of the roof upon a large warehouse. The great structure stood upon the corner, silent, bolted, and tenantless ; and all the windows, save a small round light in the upper story, were closely and securely covered with heavy shutters. Scarcely had the smoke been seen by one, when others of the crowd looked up in the same direction, and detected the unusual occurrence. Then others joined them, and still others followed, until a swelling multitude gazed upward to the roof over which the smoke soon hung like a fog ; while from eaves and shutter of the upper story little jets of black smoke burst suddenly out into the clear morning air. Then came a flash, like the lightning's glare, through the frame of the little gable window, and then another, brighter, ghastlier, and more prolonged. " Fire ! " " Fire ! " screamed the throng, as, moved by a single impulse, they pointed with excited gestures toward the window. Quicker than the time it takes to tell, the cry reached the corner, and was flashed on messenger wires to tower and steeple, engine and hose house, over the then half-sleeping city. Great bells with ponderous tongues repeated the cry with logy strokes, little bells with sharp and spiteful clicks recited the news ; while half-conscious firemen, watching through the long night, leaped upon engines and hose-carriages, and rattled into the street.

Soon the roof of the burning warehouse was drenched with floods of water, poured upon it from the hose of

many engines ; while the surging multitude in Broad
Street had grown to thousands of excited spectators.
The engines puffed and hooted, the engineers shouted,
the hook-and-ladder boys clambered upon roof and cornice, shattered the shutters and burst in the doors making way for the rescuers of merchandise and for the
surging nozzles of available hose-pipe. But the wooden
structure was a seething furnace throughout all its
upper portion ; while water and ventilation seemed only
to increase its power and fury.

"Come down ! Come down ! Off that roof ! Come
out of that building !" shouted an excited man in the
crowd, struggling with all his power in the meshes of
the solid mass of men, women, and children in the
street. "Come down ! For God's sake come down !
The rear store is filled with barrels of powder !"

"Powder !   Powder !" screamed the engineer
through his trumpet. "Powder !" shouted the horse
men. "Powder !" called the brave boys on roof and
cornice. "Powder !" answered the trumpet of the
chief. "Powder !" "Powder !" "Powder !" echoed
the menin the burning pile ; and from ladder, casement,
window, roof and cornice leaped terrified firemen with
pale faces and terror-stricken limbs.

"Push back the crowd !" shouted the engineer.
"Run for your lives ! Run ! run ! run !" roared the
trumpets of the engineers.

But, alas ! the crowd was dense and spread so far
through cross streets and alleys, that away on the out-
skirts, through the shouts of men, the whistling of the engines, and the roar of the heaven-piercing flames, the orders could not be heard. The frantic beings in front,

understanding their danger, pressed wildly back. The firemen pushed their engines and their carriages against the breasts of the crowd; but the throng moved not. So densely packed was street and square, and so various and deafening the noises, that the army of excited spectators in the rear still pressed forward with irresistible force, unconscious of danger, and regarding any outcry as a mere ruse to disperse them for convenience' sake. The great mass swayed and heaved like waves of the sea; but beyond the terrible surging of those in front, whose heart-rending screams half drowned the whistles there was no sign of retreat. As far as one could see, the streets were crowded with living human flesh and blood.

"My God! my God!" said the engineer in despair. "What can be done? Lord have mercy on us all! What can be done?"

"What can be done! I'll tell you what can be done," said one of Boston's firemen, whose hair was not yet sprinkled with gray. "Yes, *bring out* that powder! And I'm the man to do it. Better one man perish than perish all. Follow me with the water, and, if God lets me live long enough, I'll have it out."

Perhaps as the hero rushed into the burning pile, into a darkness of smoke and a withering heat, he thought of the wife and children at home, of the cheeks he had kissed in the evening, of the cheerful good-by of the prattling ones, and the laugh as he gave the "last tag;" for, as he rushed from the hoseman who tied the handkerchief over his mouth, he muttered, "God care for my little ones when I am gone." Away up through smoke and flame and cloud to the heights of heaven's throne, ascended that prayer, " God care for my little ones when I am gone," and the mighty Father and the loving Son heard the fireman's petition.

Into the flame of the rear store rushed the hero, and, groping to the barrels, rolled them speedily into the alley, where surged the stream from the engines.; rushing back and forth with power superhuman, in the deepest smoke, when even the hoops which bound the powder-barrels had already parted with fire, and while deadly harpoons loaded to pierce the whales of the Arctic seas began to explode, and while iron darts flashed by him in all directions, penetrating the walls and piercing the adjacent buildings. But as if his heroic soul was an armor-proof, or a charm impenetrable, neither harpoon nor bomb, crumbling timbers, nor showers of flaming brands, did him aught of injury, beyond the scorching of his hair and eyebrows, and the blistering of his hands and face. 'Twas a heroic deed. Did ever field of battle, wreck or martyrdom, show a braver? No act in all the list of song and story, no self-sacrifice in the history of the rise and fall of empires, was nobler than that, save one, and then the Son of God himself hung bleeding on the cross.—*R. H. Conwell.*

CALDWELL OF SPRINGFIELD.

HERE's the spot. Look around you. Above, on the height,
Lay the Hessians encamped. By that church on the right
Stood the gaunt Jersey farmers. And here ran a wall—
You may dig anywhere and you'll turn up a ball.

Nothing more, Grasses spring, waters run, flowers blow,
Pretty much as they did ninety-three years ago.

Nothing more, did I say? Stay, one moment ; you've heard
Of Caldwell, the parson, who once preached the Word
Down at Springfield? What! no? Come, that's bad ; why he
    had
All the Jerseys aflame ! and they gave him the name
Of " the rebel high priest." He stuck in their gorge,
For he loved the Lord God, and he hated King George !

He had cause, you might say ! When the Hessians that day
Marched up with Knyphausen, they stopped on their way
At the " Farms," where his wife, with a child in her arms,
Sat alone in the house. How it happened, none knew
But God, and that one of the hireling crew
Who fired the shot. Enough ! there she lay,
And Caldwell, the chaplain, her husband, away !

Did he preach—did he pray? Think of him, as you stand
By the old church, to-day ; think of him, and that band
Of militant plowboys ! See the smoke and the heat
Of that reckless advance—of that straggling retreat !
Keep the ghost of that wife, foully slain, in your view—
And what could you, what should you, what would you do ?

Why, just what he did ! They were left in the lurch
For the want of more wadding. He ran to the church,
Broke the door, stripped the pews, and dashed out in the road
With his arms full of hymn-books, and threw down his load
At their feet ! Then, above all the shouting and shots,
Rang his voice—" Put Watts into 'em, boys ! give 'em Watts ! "

And they did, That is all. Grasses spring, flowers blow,
Pretty much as they did ninety-three years ago.
You may dig anywhere and turn up a ball,
But not always a hero like this—and that's all.

                                        Bret Harte.

8

THE GLOVE AND THE LIONS.

KING FRANCIS was a hearty king, and loved a royal sport,
And one day, as his lions strove, sat looking on the court;
The nobles fill'd the benches round, the ladies by their side,
And 'mongst them Count de Lorge, with one he hoped to make
  his bride :
And truly 'twas a gallant thing to see that crowning show,
Valor and love, and a king above, and the royal beasts below.

Ramped and roared the lions, with horrid laughing jaws,
They bit, they glared, gave blows like beams, a wind went with
  their paws;
With wallowing might and stifled roar they rolled one on another
Till all the pit, with sand and mane, was in a thund'rous smother ;
The bloody foam above the bars came whizzing through the air;
Said Francis then, "Good gentlemen, we're better here than
  there ! "

De Lorge's love o'erheard the king—a beauteous, lively dame,
With smiling lips, and sharp bright eyes, which always seem'd
  the same :
She thought, " The Count, my lover, is as brave as brave can be;
He surely would do desperate things to show his love of me !
King, ladies, lovers, all look on ; the chance is wondrous fine ;
I'll drop my glove to prove his love ; great glory will be mine ! "

She dropp'd her glove to prove his love : then looked on him and
  smiled ;
He bowed, and in a moment leaped among the lions wild !
The leap was quick; return was quick; he soon regained his
  place ;
Then threw the glove, but not with love, right in the lady's face !
" Well done ! " cried Francis, " bravely done ! " and he rose from
  where he sat ·
" No love," quoth he, " but vanity, sets love a task like that ! "

Leigh Hunt.

JESSIE BROWN AT LUCKNOW.

O'ER Lucknow's wall bursts war's red thunder storm,
Round Lucknow's wall infuriate demons swarm ;
Lucknow, with men where tender women share
The siege's horrors, battling 'gainst despair ;
Where a brave few 'gainst baffled myriads strive,
Sworn not to yield, while but one man survive !
Fell hunger wastes their strength ; nearer, each day
The deadly mine works its insidious way ;—
On all sides Death stares in their doomed eyes,
Still each with each in patient courage vies :—
A few hours more must end their agonies !

A Scottish lassie, sair wi' toil oppressed,
Wrapt in her plaid, sinks down, worn out, to rest,
And says, with mind half-crazed, " Pray call me now,
As soon as Father comes home from the plough."
By night and day, with rare, unwearied zeal,
She's cheered the soldiers, brought their scanty meal,
Borne orders to the walls, the wounded nursed,
With words of comfort slaked their dying thirst :—
Now, lies she hushed amid the battle's din,
And sleeps, as if on earth there were no sin !
In dreams she wanders o'er her native hills,
Lured by the strain that Scotia's children thrills ;
And, as the much-loved notes all faintly rise,
They seem an angel-whisper from the skies !
Sudden, she starts from sleep, throws up her arms.
And listens, eager, through the war's alarms !
What new-born transport lights her sunken éye,
Flushing her pallid cheek with ecstasy ?
Entranced awhile she stands, like one inspired,
Then, wild, as if by sudden frenzy fired,
" We're saved ! " she cries ; " we're saved ! It is nae dream ;
The Highland slogan ! listen to its scream ! "—

Then to the batteries with swift step she ran,
And, in a tone that thrills each drooping man,
" Courage !" she cries, "Heav'n sends us help at last,
Hark to M'Gregor's slogan on the blast ! "
The soldiers cease their fire ; all hold their breath,
Spell-bound and fixed, a pause of life or death !
Each nerve they strain, to catch the promised sound,—
In vain !   The red artillery thunders round ;
Naught else !   Still Jessie cries in accents clear—
" The slogan's ceased ; but, hark ! dinna ye hear
The Campbell's pibroch swell upon the breeze ?
They're coming ! hark ! "—then, falling on her knees,
" We're saved !" she cries, "we're saved !   Oh, thanks to God ! "
And, fainting, sinks upon the blood-stained sod.

'Tis no girl's dream ; for, swelling on the gale,
M'Gregor's pibroch pours its piercing wail ;
That shrill, that thrilling sound, half threat, half woe,
Speaks life to us, destruction to the foe ;
Loud and more loud it grows, till strong and clear,
" Should auld acquaintance " rings upon the ear :
By solemn impulse moved, the whole host there,
Bowed in the dust, and breathed a silent prayer ;
Poured out their thanks to God in grateful tears ;
Then sprang to arms, and rent the air with cheers ;
The loyal English cheer " God save the Queen,"
The bagpipes answered with " For auld lang syne ! "
The Seventy-eighth it is ! the gallant band
Brings news that HAVELOCK is close at hand,—
The chief that never failed in hour of need,
Patient and sure, faithful in word and deed !
With glad embraces, saved and saviours meet,
Long parted comrades, comrades gayly greet ;
From every lip, on Jessie blessings pour,
Sibyl of hope, and heroine of the hour !

                                        G. Vandenhoff.

THE BATTLE OF MORGARTEN.

THE wine-month shone in its golden prime, and the red grapes clustering hung ; but a deeper sound, through the Switzer's clime, than the vintage music rung ;—a sound, through vaulted cave,—a sound, through echoing glen, like the hollow swell of a rushing wave—'twas the tread of steelgirt men ! And a trumpet, pealing wild and far, 'mid the ancient rocks was blown, till the Alps replied to that voice of war with a thousand of their own. And through the forest glooms flashed helmets to the day ; and the winds were tossing knightly plumes like pine boughs in their play. In Hasli's wilds there was gleaming steel, as the host of the Austrian passed ; and the Schreckhorn's rocks, with a savage peal, made mirth at the clarion's blast. Up 'midst the Righi snows the stormy march was heard ; with the charger's tramp, whence fire-sparks rose, and the leader's gathering word.

But a band—the noblest band of all—through the rude Morgarten strait, with blazoned streamers and lances tall, moved onwards in princely state. They came with heavy chains for the race despised so long— but amidst his Alp domains, the herdsman's arm is strong ! The sun was reddening the clouds of morn when they entered the rock defile, and shrill as a joyous hunter's horn their bugles rung the while ; but, on the misty height, where the mountain people stood, there was stillness, as of night, when storms at distance brood. There was stillness, as of deep, dead night,

and a pause—but not of fear—while the Switzers gazed
on the gathering might of the hostile shield and spear.
On wound these columns bright, between the lake and
wood; but they looked not to the misty height, where
the mountain people stood. The pass was filled with
their serried power, all helmed and mail-arrayed; and
their steps had sounds like a thunder-shower in the
rustling forest shade. There were prince and crested
knight hemmed in by cliff and flood, ... when a
shout arose from the misty height, where the mountain
people stood! And the mighty rocks come bounding
down, their startled foes among, with a joyous whirl
from the summit thrown—oh, the herdsman's arm is
strong! Like hunters of the deer, they stormed the
narrow dell; and first in the shock, with Uri's spear,
was the arm of Willian Tell! Oh, the sun in Heaven
fierce havoc viewed, when the Austrian turned to fly;
and the brave, in the trampling multitude, had a fearful
death to die! And the leader of the war at eve un-
helmed was seen, with a hurrying step on the wilds
afar, and a pale and troubled mien. But the sons of
the land which the freeman tills went back from the
battle toil, to their cabin homes, 'mid the deep green
hills, all burthened with royal spoil. There were songs
and festal fires on the soaring Alps that night, when
children sprang to meet their sires, from the wild Morgarten fight !—*Mrs. Hemans.*

HERVE RIEL.

ON the sea and at the Hogue, sixteen hundred ninety-two,
　Did the English fight the French—woe to France!
And, the thirty-first of May, helter-skelter through the blue,
Like a crowd of frightened porpoises a shoal of sharks pursue,
　Came crowding ship on ship to St. Malo on the Rance,
　　　With the English fleet in view.
'Twas the squadron that escaped, with the victor in full chase,
　First and foremost of the drove, in his great ship, Damfreville,
　　　Close on him fled, great and small,
　　　Twenty-two good ships in all;
　　　And they signaled to the place,
　　　" Help the winners of a race!
Get us guidance, give us harbor, take us quick—or, quicker
　still,
　　　Here's the English can and will!"
Then the pilots of the place put out brisk and leaped on board;
　" Why, what hope or chance have ships like these to pass?"
　laughed they;
" Rocks to starboard, rocks to port, all the passage scarred and
　scored,
Shall the ' Formidable ' here, with her twelve and eighty guns,
　Think to make the river-mouth by the single narrow way,
Trust to enter where 'tis ticklish for a craft of twenty tons,
　　　And with flow at fall beside?
　　　Now 'tis slackest ebb of tide.
　　　Reach the mooring! Rather say,
　　　While rock stands or water runs,
　　　Not a ship will leave the bay!"
　　　Then was called a council straight;
　　　Brief and bitter the debate;
" Here's the English at our heels; would you have them take in
　tow
All that's left us of the fleet, linked together stern and bow,

For a prize to Plymouth sound ?—
Better run the ships aground ! "
    (Ended Damfreville his speech),
  " Not a minute more to wait !
  Let the captains all and each
Shove ashore, then blow up, burn the vessels on the beach!
  France must undergo her fate.
  Give the word !"—But no such word
  Was ever spoke or heard;
For up stood, for out stepped, for in struck amid all these—
A captain ? A lieutenant ? A mate—first, second, third ?
  No such man of mark, and meet
  With his betters to compete !
But a simple Breton sailor pressed by Tourville for the fleet—
  A poor coasting pilot he, Hervé Riel the Croisickese.
And " What mockery or malice have we here ? " cries Hervé
  Riel ;
  " Are you mad, you Malouins ? Are you cowards, fools or
  rogues ?
Talk to me of rocks and shoals, me who took the soundings, tell
On my fingers every bank, every shallow, every swell,
  'Twixt the offing here and Grève, where the river disembogues;
Are you bought by English gold ? Is it love the lying's for ?
  Morn and eve, night and day,
  Have I piloted your bay,
Entered free and anchored fast at the foot of Solidor.
  Burn the fleet and ruin France ? That were worse than fifty
  Hogues !
  Sirs, they know I speak the truth! Sirs, believe me, there's a
  way !
  Only let me lead the line,
  Have the biggest ship to steer,
  Get this ' Formidable ' clear,
  Make the others follow mine,
And I lead them most and least by a passage I know well,
  Right to Solidor, past Grève,
  And there lay them safe and sound ;
  And if one ship misbehave—

Keel so much as grate the ground—
Why, I've nothing but my life; here's my head!" cries Hervé
Riel.
Not a minute more to wait!
"Steer us in, then, small and great!
Take the helm, lead the line, save the squadron!" cried its chief,
"Captains, give the sailor place!
He is admiral, in brief."
Still the north wind, by God's grace;
See the noble fellow's face
As the big ship, with a bound,
Clears the entry like a hound,
Keeps the passage as its inch of way were the wide sea's pro-
found!
See, safe through shoal and rock,
How they follow in a flock!
Not a ship that misbehaves, not a keel that grates the ground,
Not a spar that comes to grief!
The peril, see, is past,
All are harbored to the last,
And just as Hervé Riel hollas "Anchor!"—sure as fate,
Up the English come, too late.
So the storm subsides to calm;
They see the green trees wave
On the heights o'erlooking Grève;
Hearts that bled are stanched with balm.
"Just our rapture to enhance,
Let the English rake the bay,
Gnash their teeth and glare askance
As they cannonade away!
'Neath rampired Solidor pleasant riding on the Rance!"
Now hope succeeds despair on each captain's countenance!
Out burst all with one accord,
"This is Paradise for hell!
Let France, let France's king,
Thank the man that did the thing!"
What a shout, and all one word,
"Hervé Riel!"

As he stepped in front once more,
  Not a symptom of surprise
  In the frank blue Breton eyes—
Just the same man as before.
Then said Damfreville, " My friend,
I must speak out at the end,
  Though I find the speaking hard;
Praise is deeper than the lips,
You have saved the king his ships,
  You must name your own reward.
Faith, our sun was near eclipse !
Demand whate'er you will,
France remains your debtor still.
Ask to heart's content, and have ! or my name's not Damfreville."
  Then a beam of fun outbroke
  On the bearded mouth that spoke,
As the honest heart laughed through
Those frank eyes of Breton blue :
" Since I needs must say my say,
Since on board the duty's done,
And from Malo Roads to Croisic Point, what is it but a run ?—
  Since 'tis ask and have, I may—
  Since the others go ashore—
  Come !   A good whole holiday!
Leave to go and see my wife, whom I call the Belle Aurore !"
    That he asked, and that he got—nothing more.
  Name and deed alike are lost ;
  Not a pillar nor a post
In his Croisic keeps alive the feat as it befell :
  Not a head in white and black
  On a single fishing-smack,
In memory of the man but for whom had gone to wrack
  All that France saved from the fight whence England bore the
  bell.
    Go to Paris ; rank on rank
    Search the heroes flung pell-mell
    On the Louvre, face and flank ;
You shall look long enough ere you come to Hervé Riel.

So, for better and for worse,
Hervé Riel, accept my verse!
In my verse, Hervé Riel, do thou once more
Save the squadron, honor France, love thy wife, the Belle Aurore!
Robert Browning.

THE EXECUTION OF MONTROSE.

COME hither, Evan Cameron, come, stand beside my knee—
I hear the river roaring down towards the wintry sea.
There's shouting on the mountain-side, there's war within the
    blast;
Old faces look upon me, old forms go trooping past.
I hear the pibroch wailing amidst the din of fight,
And my dim spirit wakes again upon the verge of night.
  'Twas I that led the Highland host through wild Lochaber's
    snows,
What time the plaided clans came down to battle with Montrose.
I've told thee how the Southrons fell beneath the broad clay-
    more,
And how we smote the Campbell clan by Inverlochy's shore.
I've told thee how we swept Dundee, and tamed the Lindsay's
    pride;
But never have I told thee yet how the great Marquis died.
  A traitor sold him to his foes; oh, deed of deathless shame!
I charge thee, boy, if e'er thou meet with one of Assynt's name—
Be it upon the mountain's side, or yet within the glen,
Stand he in martial gear alone, or backed by armed men—
Face him, as thou wouldst face the man who wrong'd thy sire's
    renown;
Remember of what blood thou art, and strike the caitiff down!
  They brought him to the Watergate, hard bound with hempen
    span,
As though they held a lion there, and not a 'fenceless man.

They set him high upon a cart—the hangman rode below—
They drew his hands behind his back, and bared his noble brow.
Then, as a hound is slipp'd from leash, they cheer'd the common
    throng.
And blew the note with yell and shout, and bade him pass along.
  It would have made a brave man's heart grow sad and sick
    that day,
To watch the keen malignant eyes bent down on that array . . . .
But when he came, though pale and wan, he looked so great and
    high,
So noble was his manly front, so calm his steadfast eye,
The rabble rout forbore to shout, and each man held his breath,
For well they knew the hero's soul was face to face with death.
  But onward—always onward, in silence and in gloom,
The dreary pageant labored, till it reached the house of doom.
Then, as the Græme looked upwards, he saw the ugly smile
Of him who sold his King for gold—the master-fiend, Argyle!
And a Saxon soldier cried aloud, " Back, coward, from thy place!
For seven long years thou hast not dared to look him in the face."
  Had I been there, with sword in hand, and fifty Camerons by,
That day through high Dunedin's streets had peal'd the slogan-
    cry;
Not all their troops of trampling horse, nor might of mailed men,
Not all the rebels in the South had borne us backwards then!
Once more his foot on Highland heath had trod as free as air,
Or I, and all who bore my name, been laid around him there!
  It might not be.   They placed him next within the solemn hall,
Where once the Scottish kings were throned amidst their nobles
    all.
With savage glee came Warristoun to read the murderous doom ;
And then uprose the great Montrose in the middle of the room.
  "Now, by my faith as belted knight, and by the name I bear,
And by the bright Saint Andrew's cross that waves above us
    there,
I have not sought in battle-field a wreath of such renown,
Nor dared I hope on my dying day to win the martyr's crown!
There is a chamber far away, where sleep the good and brave,
But a better place ye have named for me, than by my father's
    grave ;

For truth and right, 'gainst treason's might, this hand hath always
striven,
And ye raise it up for a witness still, in the eye of earth and
heaven.
Then nail my head on yonder tower—give every town a limb—
And God, who made, shall gather them ; I go from you to Him !"
   Ah, boy ! that ghastly gibbet ! how dismal 'tis to see
The great, tall, spectral skeleton, the ladder and the tree !
Hark, hark ! it is the clash of arms—the bells begin to toll—
" He is coming ! he is coming ! God's mercy on his soul !"
There was color in his visage, though the cheeks of all were wan,
And they marvell'd as they saw him pass, that great and goodly
man !
He mounted up the scaffold, and he turned him to the crowd !
But they dared not trust the people, so he might not speak aloud.
But he looked upon the heavens, and they were clear and blue,
And in the liquid ether the eye of God shone through !
Yet a black and murky battlement lay resting on the hill,
As though the thunder slept within—all else was calm and still.
   The grim Geneva ministers with anxious scowl drew near,
As you have seen the ravens flock around the dying deer.
He would not deign them word nor sign, but alone he bent the
knee ;
And veil'd his face for Christ's dear grace, beneath the gallows-
tree.
Then radiant and serene he rose, and cast his cloak away ;
For he had ta'en his latest look of earth and sun and day.
   A beam of light fell o'er him, like a glory round the shriven,
And he climb'd the lofty ladder, as it were the path to heaven.
Then came a flash from out the cloud, and a stunning thunder
roll ;
And no man dared to look aloft, for fear was on every soul.
There was another heavy sound, a hush, and then a groan ;
And darkness swept across the sky—the work of death was done
                                                            Aytoun.

THE LEAP OF ROUSHAN BEG.

From the Atlantic Monthly.

MOUNTED on Kyrat strong and fleet,
His chestnut steed with four white feet,
  Roushan Beg, called Kurroglou,
Son of the road and bandit chief,
Seeking refuge and relief,
  Up the mountain pathway flew.

Such was Kyrat's matchless speed
Never yet could any steed
  Reach the dust-cloud in his course;
More than maiden, more than wife,
More than gold and next to life,
  Roushan the Robber loved his horse.

In the land that lies beyond
Erizoom and Trebizond,
  Garden-girt, his fortress stood;
Plundered khan, or caravan
Journeying north from Koordistan,
  Gave him wealth and wine and food.

Seven hundred and fourscore
Men-at-arms his livery wore,
  Did his bidding night and day;
Now through regions all unknown
He was wandering, lost, alone,
  Seeking, without guide, his way.

Suddenly the pathway ends,
Sheer the precipice descends,
  Loud the torrent roars unseen;
Thirty feet from side to side
Yawns the chasm; on air must ride
  He who crosses this ravine.

Following close in his pursuit,
At the precipice's foot,
  Reyhan the Arab of Orfah
Halted with his hundred men,
Shouting upward from the glen,
  " La il Allah !   Allah-la ! "

Gently Roushan Beg caressed
Kyrat's forehead, neck, and breast ;
  Kissed him upon both his eyes ;
Sang to him in his wild way,
As upon the topmost spray
  Sings a bird before it flies.

" Oh, my Kyrat, oh, my steed,
Round and slender as a reed,
  Carry me this danger through !
Satin housings shall be thine,
Shoes of gold, oh, Kyrat mine !
  Oh, thou soul of Kurroglou !

" Soft thy skin as silken skein,
Soft as woman's hair thy mane,
  Tender are thine eyes and true
All thy hoofs like ivory shine,
Polished bright.   Oh, life of mine,
  Leap and rescue Kurroglou ! "

Kyrat then, the strong and fleet,
Drew together his four white feet,
  Paused a moment on the verge.
Measured with his eye the space,
And into the air's embrace
  Leaped, as leaps the ocean surge.

As the surge o'er silt and sand
Bears a swimmer safe to land,
  Kyrat safe his rider bore ;
Rattling down the deep abyss,
Fragments of the precipice
  Rolled like pebbles on a shore.

Roushan's tasselled cap of red
Trembled not upon his head ;
   Careless sat he and upright ;
Neither hand nor bridle shook,
Nor his head he turned to look,
   As he galloped out of sight.

Flash of harness in the air,
Seen a moment, like the glare
   Of a sword drawn from its sheath !
Thus the phantom horseman passed ;
And the shadow that he cast
   Leaped the cataract underneath.

Reyhan the Arab held his breath
While this vision of life and death
   Passed above him. " Allah-hu ! "
Cried he ; " in all Koordistan
Breathes there not so brave a man
   As this robber Kurroglou ! "

Henry W. Longfellow.

IN THE TUNNEL.

DIDN'T know Flynn—
   Flynn of Virginia,
   Long as he's been 'yar ?
   Look 'ee here, stranger,
Whar *hev* you been ?

Here in this tunnel
   He was my pardner,
That same Tom Flynn,—
   Working together,
   In wind and weather,
Day out and in.

Didn't know Flynn!
  Well, that *is* queer;
Why, it's a sin
To think of Tom Flynn,—
  Tom with his cheer,
  Tom without fear,—
Stranger, look 'yar!

Thar in the drift,
  Back to the wall,
He held the timbers
  Ready to fall;
Then in the darkness .
  I heard him call:
" Run for your life, Jake!
Run for your wife's sake!
  Don't wait for me."
And that was all
  Heard in the din,
  Heard of Tom Flynn,—
Flynn of Virginia.

That's all about
  Flynn of Virginia.
That lets me out.
  Here in the damp,—
Out of the sun,—
  That 'ar derned lamp
Makes my eyes run.
Well, there,—I'm done!

But, sir, when you'll
Hear the next fool
  Asking of Flynn,—
Flynn of Virginia,—
  Just you chip in,
  Say you knew Flynn;
Say that you've been 'yar.

                              Bret Harte.

SUPPORTING THE GUNS.

ONE OF THE HORRORS OF WAR VIVIDLY DESCRIBED.

DID you ever see a battery take position?

It hasn't the thrill of a cavalry charge, nor the grimness of a line of bayonets moving slowly and determinedly on, but there is a peculiar excitement about it that makes old veterans rise in the saddle and cheer.

We have been fighting at the edge of the woods. Every cartridge-box has been emptied once and more, and a fourth of the brigade has melted away in dead and wounded and missing. Not a cheer is heard in the whole brigade. We know that we are being driven foot by foot, and that when we break back once more the line will go to pieces and the enemy will pour through the gap.

Here comes help!

Down the crowded highway gallops a battery, withdrawn from some other position to save ours. The field fence is scattered while you could count thirty, and the guns rush for the hill behind us. Six horses to a piece —three riders to each gun. Over dry ditches where a farmer would not drive a wagon; through clumps of bushes, over logs a foot thick, every horse on the gallop, every rider lashing his team and yelling—the sight behind us makes us forget the foe in front. The guns jump two feet high as the heavy wheels strike rock or log, but not a horse slackens his pace, not a cannoneer loses his seat. Six guns, six caissons, sixty horses, eighty men race for the brow of the hill as if he who reached it first was to be knighted.

A moment ago the battery was a confused mob. We look again and the six guns are in position, the detached horses hurrying away, the ammunition-chests open, and along our line runs the command: "Give them one more volley and fall back to support the guns!" We have scarcely obeyed when boom ! boom ! boom ! opens the battery, and jets of fire jump down and scorch the green trees under which we fought and despaired.

The shattered old. brigade has a chance to breathe for the first time in three hours as we form a line of battle behind the guns and lie down. What grim, cool fellows these cannoneers are. Every man is a perfect machine. Bullets plash dust in their faces, but they do not wince. Bullets sing over and around them, but they do not dodge. There goes one to the earth, shot through the head as he sponged his gun. The machinery loses just one beat—misses just one cog in the wheel, and then works away again as before.

Every gun is using short-fuse shell. The ground shakes and trembles—the roar shuts out all sounds from a battle-line three miles long, and the shells go shrieking into the swamp to cut trees short off—to mow great gaps in the bushes—to hunt out and shatter and mangle men until their corpses cannot be recognized as human. You would think a tornado was howling through the forest, followed by billows of fire, and yet men live through it—aye ! press forward to capture the battery ! We can hear their shouts as they form for the rush.

Now the shells are changed for grape and canister,

and the guns are served so fast that all reports blend
into one mighty roar.   The shriek of a shell is the wick-
edest sound in war, but nothing makes the flesh crawl
like the demoniac singing, purring, whistling grape-shot
and the serpent-like hiss of canister.   Men's legs and
arms are not shot through, but torn off.   Heads are
torn from bodies and bodies cut in two.   A round shot
or shell takes two men out of the ranks as it crashes
through.   Grape and canister mow a swath and pile the
dead on top each other.

Through the smoke we see a swarm of men.   It is
not a battle line, but a mob of men desperate enough
to bathe their bayonets in the flame of the guns.   The
guns leap from the ground, almost as they are depressed
on the foe, and shrieks and screams and shouts blend
into one awful and steady cry.   Twenty men out of the
battery are down, and the firing is interrupted.   The
foe accepts it as a sign of wavering, and come rushing
on.   They are not ten feet away when the guns give
them a last shot.   That discharge picks living men off
their feet and throws them into the swamp, a blackened,
bloody mass.

Up now, as the enemy are among the guns !   There
is a silence of ten seconds, and then the flash and roar
of more than 3000 muskets, and a rush forward with
bayonets.   For what ?   Neither on the right, nor left,
nor in front of us is a living foe !   There are corpses
around us which have been struck by three, four and
even six bullets, and nowhere on this acre of ground is
a wounded man !   The wheels of the guns cannot move
until the blockade of dead is removed.   Men cannot
pass from caisson to gun without climbing over winrows

of dead. Every gun and wheel is smeared with blood —every foot of grass has its horrible stain.

Historians write of the glory of war. Burial parties saw murder where historians saw glory.—*Detroit Free Press*.

PHIL BLOOD'S LEAP.

A TALE OF THE GOLD-SEEKERS.

" There's some think Injins pison. . . ." [It was Parson Pete that spoke,
As we sat there, in the camp-fire glare, like shadows among the smoke.
'Twas the dead of night, and in the light our faces shone bright red,
And the wind all round made a screeching sound and the pines roared overhead.
Aye, Parson Pete was talking: we called him Parson Pete,
For you must learn he'd a talking turn, and handled things so
. neat :
He'd a preaching style, and a winning smile, and when all talk was spent,
Six-shooter had he, and a sharp bowie, to point his argument.

Some one had spoke of the Injin folk, and we had a guess, you bet,
They might be creeping, while we were sleeping, to catch us in the net ;
And the half asleep were snoring deep, while the others vigil kept,
But devil a one let go his gun, whether he woke or slept.]

" There's some think Injins pison, and others fancy 'em scum,
And most would slay them out of the way, clean into Kingdom Come ;

But don't you go and make mistakes, like many dern'd fools I've
known,
For dirt is dirt, and snakes is snakes, but an Injin's flesh and
bone."

' We were seeking gold in the Texan hold, and we'd had a blaze of
luck,
More rich and rare the stuff ran there at every foot we struck;
Like men gone wild we toiled and toiled, and never seemed to
tire,
The hot sun glared, and our faces flared, with the greed o' gain,
like fire.

I was Captain then of the mining men, and I had a precious life,
For a wilder set I never met at derringer and at knife;
Nigh every day there was some new fray, and a shot in some one's
brain,
And the cussedest sheep in all the heap was an Imp of Sin from
Maine—

Phil Blood. Well, he was six foot three, with a squint to make
you skeer'd,
His face all scabb'd, and twisted and stabb'd, with carroty hair
and beard,
Sour as the drink in Bitter Chink, sharp as a grizzly's squeal,
Limp in one leg, for a leaden egg had nick'd him in the heel.

He was the primest workman there!—'twas a sight to see him
toil!
To the waist all bare, all devil and dare, the sweat on his cheeks
like oil;
With pickaxe and spade in sun and shade he labor'd like darna-
tion,
But when his spell was over—well! he liked recreation.

And being a crusty kind of cuss, the only sport he had
When work was over seemed to us a bit too rough and bad:

For to put some lead in a fellow's head was the greatest fun in
    life,
And the only joke he liked to poke was the point of his precious
    knife.

But game to the bone was Phil, I'll own, and he always fought
    most fair,
With as good a will to be killed as kill, true grit as any there:
Of honor, too, like me or you, he'd a scent, though not so keen,
Would rather be riddled thro' and thro', than do what he thought
    mean.

But his eddication, to his ruination, had not been over-nice,
And his stupid skull was choking full of vulgar prejudice;
For a white man *he* was an ekal, free to be fought in open fray,
But an *Injin* a snake (make no mistake) to scotch in any way.

"A sarpent's hide has pison inside, and an Injin heart's as bad—
He'll seem your friend for to gain his end, but they hate the white
    like mad;
Worse than the least of bird or beast, never at peace till dead.
A spotted snake, and no mistake!" that's what he always said,

Well, we'd jest struck our bit of luck, and were wild as raving
    men,
When who should stray to camp one day, but Black Panther, the
    Cheyenne;
Drest like a Christian, all a-grin, the old one joins our band,
And tho' the rest look'd black as sin, he shakes me by the hand.

Now the poor old cuss had been known to us, and I knew that
    he was true—
I'd have trusted him with life and limb as soon as I'd trust *you;*
For tho' his wit was gone a bit, and he drank like any fish,
His heart was kind, he was well inclined as even a white could
    wish.

Food had got low, for we didn't know the run of the hunting-
    ground,
And our hunters were sick, when, just in the nick, the friend in
    need was found;

For he knew the place like his mother's face (or better, a heap, you'd say,

Since she was a squaw of the roaming race, and himself a cast-away).

Well, I took the Panther into camp, and the critter was well content,

And off with him, on the hunting tramp, next day our party went;

And I reckon that day and the next we didn't hunger for food,

And only one in the camp look'd vext—that Imp of Sin—Phil Blood.

Nothing would please his contrairy idees! an Injin made him boil!

But he said nought, and his scowling wrought from morn till night at his toil.

And I knew his skin was hatching sin, and I kept the Panther apart,

For the Injin he was too weak to see the depths of a white man's heart!

One noon-day when myself and the men were resting by the creek,

The red sun blazed, and we lay half dazed, too tired to stir or speak,

'Neath the alder trees we stretched at ease, and we couldn't see the sky,

For the lian-flowers in bright blue showers hung through the branches high.

It was like the gleam of a fairy-dream, and I felt like earth's first Man,

In an Eden bower with the yellow flower of a cactus for a fan;

Oranges, peaches, grapes and figs cluster'd, ripen'd and fell,

And the cedar scent was pleasant, blent with the soothing 'cacia smell.

The squirrels red ran overhead, and I saw the lizards creep,

And the woodpecker bright with the chest so white tapt like a sound in sleep;

I lay and dozed with eyes half closed, and felt like a three-year
child,
And, a plantain blade on his brow for a shade, even Phil Blood
look'd mild.

Well, back jest then came our hunting men, with the Panther at
their head,
Full of his fun was every one, and the Panther's eyes were red,
And he skipt about with grin and shout, for he'd had a drop that
day,
And he twisted and twirled, and squeal'd and skirl'd, in the fool-
ish Injin way.

To the waist all bare Phil Blood lay there, with only his knife in
his belt,
And I saw his bloodshot eye-balls flare, and I knew how fierce he
felt,
When the Injin dances with grinning glances around him as he
lies,
With his painted skin and his monkey grin—and leers into his eyes.

Then before I knew what I should do Phil Blood was on his
feet,
And the Injin could trace the hate in his face, and his heart began to beat,
And "Get out o' the way," he heard them say, "for he means to
hev your life!"
But before he could fly at the warning cry, he saw the flash of
the knife.

"Run, Panther, run!" cried every one, and the Panther took
the track,
With a wicked glare, like a wounded bear, Phil Blood sprang at
his back.
Up the side so steep of the canon deep the poor old critter sped,
And after him ran the devil's limb till they faded overhead.

Now the spot of ground where our luck was found was a queer-
ish place, you'll mark,
Jest under the jags of the mountain crags and the precipices dark,

And the water drove from a fall above, and roared both day and
    night,
And those that waded beneath were shaded by crags to left and
    right.

Far up on high, close to the sky, the two crags leant together,
Leaving a gap like an open trap, with a gleam of golden weather,
And now and then when at work the men lookt up they caught
    the bounds
Of the deer that leap from steep to steep, and they seemed the
    size o' hounds.

A pathway led from the deck's dark bed up to the crags on high,
And up that path the Injin fled, fast as a man could fly.
Some shots were fired, for I desired to keep the white cuss back ;
But I missed my man, and away he ran on the flying Injin's track.

Now all below is thick, you know, with 'cacia, alder and pine,
And the bright shrubs deck the side of the beck, and the lian-
    flowers so fine,
For the forests creeps all under the steeps, and feathers the feet
    of the crags
With boughs so thick that your path you pick, like a steamer
    among the snags.

But right above you, the crags, Lord love you! are bare as this
    here hand,
And your eyes you wink at the bright blue chink, as looking up
    you stand.
If a man should pop in that trap at the top, he'd never rest hand
    or leg,
Till neck and crop to the bottom he'd drop—and smash on the
    stones like an egg !

Now the breadth of the trap, tho' it seemed so small from the
    place below, d'ye see,
Was what a deer could easily clear, but a man—well, not for *me!*
And it happened, yes ! the path, I guess, led straight to that there
    place,
And if one of the two didn't leap it, whew ! they must meet there
    face to face.

"Come back, you cuss! come back to us! and let the critter be!"
I screamed out loud, while the men in a crowd stood gazing at
    them and me;
But up they went, and my shots were spent, and I shook as they
    disappeared—
One minute more and we gave a roar, for the Injin had leapt—
    and *cleared!*

A leap for a deer, not a man, to clear—and the bloodiest grave
    below!
But the critter was smart, and mad with fear, and he went like a
    bolt from a bow!
Close after him came the devil's limb, with his eyes as wild as
    death,
But when he came to the gulch's brim I reckon he paused for
    breath!

For breath at the brink! but—a white man shrink, when a red
    had passed so neat?
I knew Phil Blood too well to think he'd turn his back dead beat!
He takes one run, leaps up in the sun, and bounds from the slip-
    pery ledge,
And he clears the hole, but—God help his soul! just touches the
    other edge!

One scrambling fall, one shriek, one call from the men that stand
    and stare—
Black in the blue where the sky looks thro', he staggers, dwarf'd
    up there;
The edge he touches, then sinks, and clutches the rock—my eyes
    grow dim—
I turn away—what's that they say?—he's a-hanging on to the
    brim!

. . . On the very brink of the fatal chink a wild thin shrub there
    grew,
And to that he clung, and in silence swung betwixt us and the
    blue,

And as soon as a man could run I ran the way I'd seen them flee,
And I came mad-eyed to the chasm's side, and—what do you
  think I see?

All up? Not quite. Still hanging? Right! But he'd torn
  away the shrub;
With lolling tongue he clutch'd and swung—to what? aye, that's
  the rub!
I saw him glare and dangle in air—for the empty hole he trode—
Help'd by a *pair of hands* up there! The Injin's? Yes, by —— !

Now, boys, look here! for many a year I've roughed in this here
  land,
And many a sight both day and night I've seen that I think
  grand;
Over the whole wide world I've been, and I know both things and
  men,
But the biggest sight I've ever seen was the sight I saw just then.

I held my breath—so nigh to death the cuss swung hand and
  limb,
And it seem'd to me that down he'd flee, with the Panther after
  him:
But the Injin at length puts out his strength, and another minute
  past,
And safe and sound to the solid ground he drew Phil Blood at
  last!

Saved? True for you! By an Injin too!—and the man he meant
  to kill!
There all alone, on the brink of stone, I see them standing still;
Phil Blood gone white, with the struggle and fright, like a great
  mad bull at bay,
And the Injin meanwhile, with a half-skeer'd smile, ready to
  spring away.

What did Phil do? Well, I watched the two, and I saw Phil
  Blood turn back,
Then he leant to the brink and took a blink into the chasm black,

Then, stooping low for a moment or so, he drew his bowie bright,
And he chucked it down the gulf with a frown and whistle, and
lounged from sight.

Hands in his pockets, eyes downcast, silent, thoughtful and grim,
While the Panther, grinning as he passed, still kept his eyes on
him;
Phil Blood strolled slow to his mates below, down by a mountain
track,
With his lips set tight and his face all white, and the Panther at
his back.

I reckon they stared when the two appeared! but never a word
Phil spoke—
Some of them laughed and others jeered—but he let them have
their joke;
He seemed amazed, like a man gone dazed, the sun in his eyes too
bright,
And, in spite of their cheek for many a week, he never offered to
fight.

And after that day he changed his play, and kept a civiler tongue,
And whenever an Injin came that way, his contrairy head he
hung;
But whenever he heard the lying word, " *It's a* LIE ! " Phil Blood
would groan ;
" *A snake is a snake, make no mistake ! but an Injin's flesh and
bone !* "

Robert Buchanan.

KATE MALONEY.

IN the winter, when the snowdrift stood against the cabin door,
Kate Maloney, wife of Patrick, lay nigh dying on the floor—
Lay on rags and tattered garments, moaning out with feeble
breath,
"Knale beside me, Pat, my darlint ; pray the Lord to give me
death."

Patrick knelt him down beside her, took her thin and wasted
    hand,
Saying something to her softly that she scarce could understand.
"Let me save ye, oh, my honey! Only spake a single word,
And I'll sell the golden secret where its wanted to be heard.

"Sure it cuts my heart to see ye lyin' dyin' day by day,
When it's food and warmth ye're wanting just to dhrive yer pains
    away.
There's a hundred goolden guineas at my mercy if ye will—
Do ye know that Mickey Regan's in the hut upon the hill?

Kate Maloney gripped her husband, then she looked him through
    and through;
"Pat Maloney, am I dhraming? Did I hear them words o' you?
Have I lived an honest woman, lovin' Ireland, God and thee,
That now upon my death-bed ye should spake them words to
    me?

"Come, ye here, ye tremblin' traitor; stand beside me now, and
    swear
By yer soul and yer hereafter, while he lives ye will not dare
Whisper e'en a single letter o' brave Mickey Regan's name.
Can't I die o' cold and hunger? Would ye have me die o' shame?

"Let the Saxon bloodhounds hunt him, let them show their filthy
    gold;
What's the poor boy done to hurt 'em? Killed a rascal rich and
    old—
Shot an English thief who robbed us, grinding Irish peasants
    down;
Raisin rints to pay his wontons and his lackeys up in town.

"We are beasts, we Irish peasants, whom these Saxon tyrants
    spurn;
If ye hunt a beast too closely, and ye wound him, won't he turn?
Wasn't Regan's sister ruined by the blackguard lying dead,
Who was paid his rint last Monday, not in silver, but in lead?"

Pat Maloney stood and listened, then he knelt and kissed his wife :
"Kiss me, darlint, and forgive me; sure, I thought to save your
    life ;
And it's hard to see ye dyin' when the gold's within my reach,
I'll be lonely when ye're gone, dear—" here a whimper stopped
    his speech.

                *   *   *   *   *   *   *   *

Late that night, when Kate was dozing, Pat crept cautiously
    away
From his cabin to the hovel where the hunted Regan lay ;
He was there—he heard him breathing, something whispered to
    him "Go!—
Go and claim the hundred guineas—Kate will never need to
    know."

He would plan some little story when he brought her food to
    eat,
He would say the priest had met him, and had sent her wine
    and meat.
No one passed their lonely cabin ; Kate would lie and fancy still
Mick had slipped away in secret from the hut upon the hill.

Kate Maloney woke and missed him ; guessed his errand there
    and then ;
Raised her feeble voice and cursed him with the curse of God
    and men.
From her rags she slowly staggered, took her husband's loaded
    gun,
Crying, "God, I pray Thee, help me, ere the traitor's deed be
    done ! "

All her limbs were weak with fever as she crawled across the
    floor ;
But she writhed and struggled bravely till she reached the cabin
    door ;
Thence she scanned the open country, for the moon was in its
    prime,
And she saw her husband running, and she thought, " There yet is
    time."

He had come from Regan's hiding, past the door, and now he
    went
By the pathway down the mountain, on his evil errand bent.
Once she called him, but he stopped not, neither gave he glance
    behind,
For her voice was weak and feeble, and it melted on the wind.

Then a sudden strength came to her, and she rose and followed
    fast,
Though her naked limbs were frozen by the bitter winter blast;
She had reached him very nearly when her newborn spirit fled.
"God has willed it!" cried the woman, *then she shot the traitor
    dead!*

From her bloodless lips, half frozen, rose a whisper to the sky—
"I have saved his soul from treason; here, O Heaven, let me die.
Now no babe unborn shall curse him, nor his country loathe his
    name;
I have saved ye, oh, my husband, from a deed of deathless shame."

No one yet has guessed their story; Mickey Regan got away,
And across the kind Atlantic lives an honest man to-day;
While in Galway still the peasants show the lonely mountain
    side
Where an Irishman was murdered and an Irishwoman died.

                                Dagonet.

TOM.

YES, Tom's the best fellow that ever you knew.
      Just listen to this:
When the old mill took fire, and the flooring fell through,
And I with it, helpless there, full in my view,
What do you think my eyes saw through the fire,
That crept along, crept along, nigher and nigher,
But Robin, my baby-boy, laughing to see
The shining! He must have come there after me,

Toddled alone from the cottage without
Any one's missing him. Then, what a shout—
Oh, how I shouted, " For Heaven's sake, men,
Save little Robin!" Again and again
They tried, but the fire held them back like a wall.
I could hear them go at it, and at it, and call,
" Never mind, baby, sit still like a man,
We're coming to get you as fast as we can."
They could not see him, but I could; he sat
Still on a beam, his little straw hat
Carefully placed by his side, and his eyes
Stared at the flame with a baby's surprise,
Calm and unconscious as nearer it crept.
The roar of the fire up above must have kept
The sound of his mother's voice shrieking his name
From reaching the child. But *I* heard it. It came
Again and again—O God, what a cry!
The axes went faster, I saw the sparks fly
Where the men worked like tigers, nor minded the heat
That scorched them—when, suddenly, there at their feet
The great beams leaned in—they saw him—then, crash,
Down came the wall! The men made a dash—
Jumped to get out of the way—and I thought
" All's up with poor little Robin," and brought
Slowly the arm that was least hurt to hide
The sight of the child there, when swift, at my side,
Some one rushed by, and went right through the flame
Straight as a dart—caught the child—and then came
Back with him—choking and crying, but—saved!
Saved safe and sound!
                    Oh, how the men raved,
Shouted, and cried, and hurrahed? Then they all
Rushed at the work again, lest the back wall
Where I was lying, away from the fire,
Should fall in and bury me.
                    Oh, you'd admire
To see Robin now; he's as bright as a dime,
Deep in some mischief, too, most of the time;

10

Tom, it was, saved him.   Now isn't it true,
Tom's the best fellow that ever you knew?
There's Robin now—see, he's strong as a log—
And there comes Tom too—
                    Yes, Tom was our dog.
                              Constance Fenimore Woolson.

THE DIVER.

TRANSLATED BY J. C. MAGAN.

" BARON or vassal, is any so bold
    As to plunge in yon gulf, and follow,
Through chamber and cave, this beaker of gold—
    Which already the waters whirlingly swallow?
Who retrieves the prize from the horrid abyss
    Shall keep it : the gold and the glory be his!"
So spake the king, and, incontinent flung
    From the cliff, that, gigantic and steep,
High over Charybdis's whirlpool hung,
    A glittering wine-cup down in the deep;
And again he asked: "Is there one so brave
    As to plunge for the gold in the dangerous wave?"
And the knights and the knaves all answerless hear
    The challenging words of the speaker;
And some glanced downward with looks of fear,
    And none are ambitious of winning the beaker.
And a third time the king his question urges—
    "Dares none, then, breast the menacing surges?
But the silence lasts unbroken and long;
    When a page, fair-featured and soft,
Steps forth from the shuddering vassal-throng,
    And his mantle and girdle already are doffed,
And the groups of nobles and damsels nigh
    Envisage the youth with a wondering eye.

He dreadlessly moves to the gaunt crag's brow,
  And measures the drear depth under ;—
But the waters Charybdis had swallowed, she now
  Regurgitates, bellowing back in thunder ;
And the foam, with a stunning and horrible sound,
  Breaks its hoar way through the waves around.
And it seethes and roars, it welters and boils,
  As when water is showered upon fire ;
And skyward the spray agonizingly toils,
  And flood over flood sweeps higher and higher,
Upheaving, downrolling, tumultuously,
  As though the abyss would bring forth a young sea.
And now, ere the din rethunders, the youth
  Invokes the great name of GOD ;
And blended shrieks of horror and ruth
  Burst forth as he plunges headlong unawed ;
And down he descends through the watery bed,
  And the waves boom over his sinking head.
Now, wert thou even, O Monarch ! to fling
  Thy crown in the angry abyss,
And exclaim, " Who recovers the crown shall be king ! "
  The guerdon were powerless to tempt me, I wis ;
For what in Charybdis's caverns dwells
  No chronicle penned of mortal tells.
Full many a vessel beyond repeal
  Lies low in that gulf to-day,
And the shattered masts and the drifting keel
  Alone tell the tale of the swooper's prey.
But hark !—with a noise like the howling of storms,
  Again the wild water the surface deforms.
When lo ! ere as yet the billowy war,
  Loud raging beneath, is o'er,
An arm and a neck are distinguished afar—
  And a swimmer is seen to make for the shore ;
And hardily buffeting surge and breaker,
  He springs upon land, with the golden beaker.
And lengthened and deep is the breath he draws,
  As he hails the bright face of the sun ;

And a murmer goes round of delight and applause.
He lives!—he is safe!—he has conquered and won!
He has mastered Charybdis's perilous wave!
He has rescued his life and his prize from the grave!
Now, bearing the booty triumphantly,
 At the foot of the throne he falls,
And he proffers his trophy on bended knee;
 And the king to his beautiful daughter calls,
Who fills with red wine the golden cup,
 While the gallant stripling again stands up,
" All hail to the King! Rejoice, ye who breathe,
 Wheresoever Earth's gales are driven!
For ghastly and drear is the region beneath;
 And let man beware how he tempts high Heaven!
Let him never essay to uncurtain to light
 What destiny shrouds in horror and night.
The maelstrom dragged me down in its course;
 When, forth from the cleft of a rock,
A torrent outrushed with tremendous force,
 And met me anew with deadening shock;
And I felt my brain swim and my senses reel,
 As the double flood whirled round me like a wheel.
But the GOD I had cried to answered me
 When my destiny darkliest frowned,
And he showed me a reef of rocks in the sea,
 Whereunto I clung, and there I found
On a coral jag the goblet of gold,
 Which else to the lowermost crypt had rolled.
And the gloom through measureless toises under
 Was all in a purple haze;
And though sound was none in these realms of wonder,
 I shuddered when under my shrinking gaze
That wilderness lay developed, where wander
 The dragon, the dog-fish and sea-salamander.
And there I hung, aghast and dismayed,
 Among skeleton larvæ; the only
Soul conscious of life—despairing of aid
 In that vastness untrodden and lonely.

Not a human voice—not an earthly sound—
But silence, and water, and monsters around !
Soon one of these monsters approached me, and plied
   His hundred feelers to drag
Me down to the darkness, when, springing aside,
   I abandoned my hold of the coral crag.
And the maelstrom grasped me with arms of strength,
And upwhirled and upbore me to daylight at length."
Then spake to the page the marvelling king—
   " The golden cup is thine own,
But—I promise thee further this jewelled ring,
That beams with a priceless hyacinth stone,
Should'st thou dive once more, and discover for me
The mysteries shrined in the cells of the sea."
Now, the king's fair daughter was touched and grieved,
   And she fell at her father's feet—
" O father ! enough what the youth has achieved !
   Expose not his life anew, I entreat !
If this your heart's longing you cannot well tame,
There are surely knights here who will rival his fame."
But the king hurled downwards the golden cup ;
   And spake as it sank in the wave—
" Now, should'st thou a second time bring it me up,
   As my knight, and the bravest of all my brave,
Thou shalt sit at my nuptial banquet, and she
Who pleads for thee thus thy wedded shall be ! "
Then the blood to the youth's hot temples rushes,
   And his eyes on the maiden are cast,
And he sees her at first overspread with blushes,
   And then growing pale, and sinking aghast ;
So, vowing to win so glorious a crown,
For life, or for death, he again plunges down !
The far-sounding din returns amain,
   And the foam is alive as before,
And all eyes are bent downward.   In vain ! in vain !
   The billows indeed re-dash and re-roar ;
But while ages shall roll, and those billows shall thunder,
That youth shall sleep under !

                          Schiller.

FATHER JOHN.

HE warn't no long-faced man o' prayer,
 A-peddlin' scriptures here and there,
A-shootin' off his texts and tracts
Without regard to dates and facts
Or time or place, like all possessed,
'Till weary sinners couldn't rest;
Fatiguin' unregenerate gents,
And causin' molls to swear immense.
He didn't snivel worth a cent,
Nor gush to any great extent,
But labored on a level plan—
A priest, but none the less a man—
Among the slums and boozing-kens,
And in the vilest holes and dens,
Amongst the drabs and owls and worse—
For saints in these here parts are skerce;
This ward ain't nowadays flush o' them,
It ain't no new Jerusalem.
He preached but little, argued less:
But if a moll was in distress,
Or if a kinchen came to grief,
Or trouble tackled rogue or thief,
There Father John was sure to be,
To blunt the edge o' misery;
And somehow managed every time
To ease despair or lessen crime.
That corner house was allus known
Around these parts as Podger's Own,
'Till two pams in a druken fight
Set the whole thing afire one night;
And where it stood they hypered round
And blasted rocks and shovelled ground
To build the factory over there—
The one you see—and that is where

Poor Father John—God give him rest !—
Preached his last sermon and his best.
One summer's day the thing was done ;
The workmen set a blast and run.
They ain't so keerful here, I guess,
Where lives ain't worth a cent apiece,
As in the wards where things is dear,
And nothink ain't so cheap as here ;
Leastwise the first they seed or knowed
A little chick had crossed the road,
He seemed to be just out o' bed,
Barelegged, with nothink on his head;
Chubby and cunnin', with his hair
Blown criss-cross by the mornin' air ;
Draggin' a tin horse by a string,
Without much care for anything,
A talking to hisself for joy—
A toddlin', keerless baby boy.
Right for the crawlin' fuse he went,
As though to find out what it meant;
Trudgin' towards the fatal spot,
'Till less'n three feet off he got
From where the murderin' thing lay still,
Just waitin' for to spring and kill ;
Marching along toward his grave,
And not a soul dared go to save.
They hollered—all they durst to do ;
He turned and laughed, and then bent low
To set the horsey on his feet,
And went right on, a crowin' sweet,
And then a death-like silence grew
On all the tremblin', coward crew,
As each swift second seemed the last
Before the roaring of the blast.
Just then some chance or purpose brought
The priest; he saw, and quick as thought
He ran and caught the child, and turned
Just as the slumberin' powder burned.

And shot the shattered rocks around,
And with its thunder shook the ground.
The child was sheltered; Father John
Was hurt to death; without a groan
He set the baby down, then went
A step or two, but life was spent;
He tottered, looked up to the skies
With ashen face, but strange, glad eyes.
"My love, I come!" was all he said,
Sank slowly down, and so was dead.
Stranger, he left a memory here
That will be felt for many a year,
And since that day this ward has been
More human in its dens of sin.

Peleg Arkwright.

DEATH OF "OLD BRAZE."

From the "Detroit Free Press."

SOME boys came down to No. 1's house and reported that old Braze was going to die. Several of the men went to his little old shanty on Macomb Street, fearing that the report was true, and sorry that the old man's time had finally come, although he had little to live for.

Braze used to run with a hand machine in the long ago, and he never felt quite right about the steamers coming here to break up fire companies and destroy time-honored customs. The clank of the fire-bell would rouse him even after he was old and bent and feeble, and he would creep down to the fire and cheer as the pipemen dashed into the smoke and flames, and as the hook and ladder boys hung to the cornices, and passed in and out of the windows. He didn't say a word against the puffing, powerful steamers, but he longed for the days when No. 6 and No. 10 and No. 3 took water from the same cistern, and when the " Break 'er down, boys!" of the foreman drowned the roar of the flames. He used to come down to No. 1's house and sit for hours at a time, and finally came to consider himself a member of the Department, although he couldn't quite get over the loss of drag-ropes, trumpets, red shirts, and a company fight now and then.

Loneliness, poverty and want met the eyes of the visitors as they entered the little old house. Old Braze was lying on a miserable bed; and a ragged boy, who had been sent in by a neighbor to keep the old man company, had grown weary and fallen asleep in his chair.

" I sent you word, boys, because I'm going out of commission to-day!" said the old man to the firemen. " Yes, this old machine is worn out, and she's to be laid up!"

On the wall over his head was a fireman's leather hat; across the room hung a battered brass trumpet with its faded cord and tassels. Not a picture—not an ornament—bare walls, with here and there a spot through which one could see daylight. He had lived alone for years, and he had become used to the gloom and wretchedness and the poverty. Death had already set its seal upon the old man's face, and the firemen had not come an hour too soon.

" Get any alarms last night?" he asked, as the men sat around him.

" It had been a quiet night," they said.

"It's kinder tough to be laid away where a feller can't hear the bells!" continued the old man, "and it seems as if he'd be lonesome! I s'pose there'll be general alarms, and big fires, and all the steamers out, and I won't know anything about it."

One of them asked him if he didn't want to see a clergyman.

"No, I guess not," he replied. "I've been praying a little this morning, and kinder thinking over old days, forgiving everybody and asking forgiveness. When I'm gone, I'd like to have you boys man the brakes, and put me under the sod in sort o' decent style."

They asked what should be done with his personal effects, and he replied:

"I'd like the hat and trumpet put into the coffin along with me; seems as if I'd rest better for knowing they were there. The neighbors can come in and take away the rest."

After a few minutes his mind began to wander, and he whispered to himself. Then he shook off the weakness, and trying hard to discern the faces of the men through the glaze of death, he asked:

"Isn't that an alarm?"

They smoothed back his thin, gray hair, and whispered that he was mistaken.

"I thought it struck box 421," he went on after a moment; "but I s'pose death's picked up the drag-rope, and is hauling me out of the house."

He was quiet again for two or three minutes, and then drew himself up, looked wildly around, and whispered:

"Tell No. 7 to play through two hundred feet of hose !"

They tried to lay him down, but he pushed them away and hoarsely shouted :

"Down with the brakes—chuck'er, boys; hi! hi— h-a-a-a !"

He fell back, and the boy, roused by his words, sprang off the chair, and after a glance at the white face on the bed, he whispered : "Why, old Braze is dead !"

And he was.—*Anon.*

Burdett's Dramatic Recitations and Readings.

Compiled and arranged for Reading, Speaking, Recitations and Elecutionary exercises.

CONTENTS.

Baron's Last Banquet, The.
Benediction, The.
Boat-Race, The.
Death.
Death-bed of Benedict Arnold.
Death of the Drunkard, The.
Death of King John.
Death of Murat.
Death of the Old Squire, The.
Death of the Reveller, The.
Dream of Eugene Aram, The.
Dying Hebrew, The.
Education.
Evangelist, The.
Fearless DeCourcy, The.
Flight for Life, The.
Forgive,—No, Never.
Forgotten Actor, The.
Galley-Slave, The.
Game Knut Played, The.
Ivan, The Czar.
Jean Goëllo's Yarn.
King Robert of Sicily.
Last Banquet, The.
Legend of the Church of Los Angeles, A.
Legend of a Veil.
Leper, The.
Little Ned.
"Lynch for Lynch."
Mary Queen of Scots.
Marseillaise at Sebastopol, The.
Mask and Domino.
Night Watch, The.
Ode to Eloquence.
O Maria, Regina Misericordiæ.
One of King Charles' Madcap Men.
Painter of Florence, The.
Parrhasius.
Portrait, The.
Ramon.
Rescue, The.
Richelieu; or, the Conspiracy.
Sea Captain's Story, The.
Spanish Page, The.
Three Words (The), Arnold, the Traitor.
Tiger Bay.
Told at the Falcon.
Two Loves and a Life.

Bound in illuminated paper cover. - - - - **Price, 25 cents.**

BURDETT'S NEGRO DIALECT RECITATIONS AND HUMOROUS READINGS.

Containing the latest and best hints of modern Negro Ministrelsy, being by far the most perfect book of its kind ever published.

CONTENTS.

An Examination in History.
Apples: an Original Negro Lecture.
Bad Churchman, A.
Blind Ned.
Brother Anderson.
Brother Gardner and Judge Cadaver.
Brother Gardner on Music.
Brudder Bones's Love Scrape.
Brudder Plato Johnson's Sermon.
"Business" in Mississippi.
Cæsar Rowan.
Christmas Baby, The.
Christmas Night in the Quarters.
Colored Preacher's Religious Experience, A.
Darky Bootblack, The.
Darky Preacher, The.
Darky's Story, The.
De Cake Walk.
Devil's Ride, The.
First Banjo, The.
Half-Way Doings.
How Persimmons Took Cah ob de Baby.
Kentucky Philosophy.
Mahsr John.
Marcellino's Conversion.
Marriage a Mighty Serious Thing.
Momma Phœbe.
Negro Aphorisms.
"Nigger Made Happy."
"No Party To-Night."
Old Daddy Turner.
Old Hostler's Experience, The.
"Ole Man's" Lament, The.
Old Sambo Puzzled.
Old Si Pilots a 'Possum Hunt.
Parson Snow's Broad Hint.
Pine Town Darky Debating Society, The.
Plantation Song, A.
Precepts at Parting.
Professor Barbour's Experiment.
Rev. Plato Johnson Visits New York, The.
Rev. Uncle Jim's Sermon, The.
Sambo's Dilemma.
Sam's Feast.
Ship of Faith, The.
Sollum Fac', A.
Sunday Fishin'.
Teco Brag's Lecture.
Ter'ble 'Sperience, A.
Terpsichore in the Flat Creek Quarters.
Three Wishes, The.
Uncle Anderson on Prosperity.
Uncle Billy and the Civil Rights Bill.
Uncle Eph Kimble's Mistake.
Uncle Gabe's White Folks.
Uncle Ike's Roosters.
Uncle Joel.
Uncle Ned's Defence.
Uncle Pete and Marse George.
Uncle Reuben's Baptism.
War of Races, The.
"Whar's de Kerridge?"
What's a Dolla to a Man wid a Family
What Troubled the Nigger.
Wounded in the Corners.

Bound in illuminated paper cover. - - - - **Price, 25 cents.**

For sale by all Booksellers, or will be sent, post-paid, on receipt of price.

EXCELSIOR PUBLISHING HOUSE,

P. O. Box 1144.   **29 and 31 Beekman Street, New York, N. Y.**

BURDETT'S
Patriotic Recitations and Readings.

A carefully compiled collection of Patriotic recitals, designed and arranged for Public or Parlor Reading.

CONTENTS.

After the Battle.
America.
American Flag, The.
Arnold Winkleried.
Barbara Frietchie.
Battle of Fort Moultrie, The.
Battle-Flag at Shenandoah, The.
Battle of Bunker Hill.
Battle of Lexington, The.
Battle of Lookout Mountain, The.
Battle of Gettysburg, The.
Battle-Flags, The.
"Bay Billy."
Bivouac of the Dead, The.
Blue and the Gray, The.
Boston Boys.
Caldwell of Springfield.
Capture of Stony Point, The.
Charge by the Ford, The.
Columbia.
Conquered Banner, The.
Decoration Day.
Drafted.
Duty of the American Scholar.
E Pluribus Unum.
Ensign-Bearer, The.
Foes United in Death.
Fourth of July.
Georgia Volunteer, The.
Gun of New Orleans, The.
John Burns of Gettysburg.
Kearny at Seven Pines.
Kelly's Ferry.

Kentucky Belle.
Little Regiment, The.
Lookout Mountain, 1863.
Miles Keogh's Horse.
Nation's Hymn, The.
Nation's Dead, The.
Old Sergeant, The.
Old Soldier's Story, The.
Old Surgeon's Story, The.
Old Soldier Tramp, The.
Old Canteen, The.
One in Blue and One in Gray.
Opposition to Misgovernment.
Our Whole Country.
Our Country.
Our Heroes.
Paul Revere's Ride.
Patriotism.
Patriot Spy, The.
Pride of Battery B, The.
Revolutionary Rising, The.
Saving of the Colors, The.
Scott and the Veteran.
Sheridan's Ride.
Somebody's Darling.
Sprig of Green, The.
Stars and Stripes, The.
Substitute, The.
Sword of Bunker Hill, The.
Tribute to our Honored Dead, A.
Union and Liberty.
Union of the States, The.
Union Linked with Liberty.

Bound in illustrated paper cover. **Price, 25 cents.**

For sale by all Booksellers, or will be sent, post-paid, on receipt of price.

EXCELSIOR PUBLISHING HOUSE,
29 and 31 Beekman Street, New York, N. Y.
P. O. Box 1144.

Excelsior Recitations *and* Readings

NO. 3. CONTENTS:

Asleep at the Switch.
Battle of Waterloo, The.
Benediction.
Biddy Maginness at the Photographer's.
Billy's Rose.
Black Horse and his Rider, The.
Book Canvasser, The.
Brier Rose.
Californian and a New York Segar, A.
Caoch the Piper.
Cataract of Lodore, The.
Catawba Wine.
Children We Keep. The.
Chinese Excelsior, The.
Clothing Business, The.
Coals of Fire.
Como.
Curfew Must Not Ring To-Night.
Death of Robespierre, The.
Difficulty in Rhyming.
Farmer John.
Fearless De Courcy, The.
Flash. (The Fireman Story.)
Fly Cogitation, A.
Going to School.
Granger and the Gambler, The.
Her Rival.
How Girls Study.
How Jane Conquest Rang the Bell.
Jack.
Kitchen Clock, The.
Left.

Life Boat, The.
Life's Magnet.
Mary's Lamb on a New Principle.
Maud Rosihue's Choice.
Miss Maloney on the Chinese Question.
Moll Jarvis O'Marley.
Mrs. Smart Learns How to Skate.
My Garden.
My Lover.
Nancy.
Now and Then.
Old Man in the Palace Car, The.
Our Travelled Parson.
Phryne's Husband.
Poor-House Man.
Bevenge is Sweet.
Room Enough for All.
Scandal, A.
Seedy One, A. (A Tale of Fraud and Deception.)
Sign-Board, The.
Sister of Charity, The.
Smoker's Soliloquy, A.
Tale of a Dog, The.
To a Skeleton.
Trouble in the Amen Corner.
Uncle Ned's Defence.
Valentine, The.
What is a Gentleman?
When.
Witness, The.
Wounded.
Wrong Train, The.

176 Pages, Paper Cover...............Price 25 cents.

WILSON'S
Ball-Room Guide;
OR,
DANCING SELF-TAUGHT.

The latest and most complete of any publication of its kind out, embracing not only the whole theory and practice of Terpsichorean Art, but full and requisite information for the giving of RECEPTIONS, PARTIES, BALLS, etc., from the commencement to the ending, with clear directions for CALLING OUT THE FIGURES OF EVERY DANCE, and a host of other matters, all expressed in plain language, added to which are clear and practical instruction diagrams of marches, forms of invitations, programmes, etc., together with thirty-eight pages of the latest and most fashionable COPYRIGHT MUSIC, never before issued in book form, making this book the most thorough and complete publication on dancing ever issued.

Bound in Illuminated Board Cover, with Cloth back. Price 75 cents.

Bound in Illuminated Paper Cover. Price 50 cents.

How to Draw and Paint.

A Complete Handbook on the whole art of Drawing and Painting, containing concise instructions in

OUTLINE, LIGHT AND SHADE, PERSPECTIVE, SKETCHING FROM NATURE; FIGURE DRAWING, ARTISTIC ANATOMY, LANDSCAPE, MARINE, AND PORTRAIT PAINTING;

the principles of Colors applied to Paintings, etc., etc., with over 100 Illustrations.

12mo, boards, with cloth back.   Price 50 cents.

It must be of great service to all teachers and students of drawing and painting.—*Davenport (Iowa) Daily Gazette.*

It certainly seems to us the best work of the kind we have met with.—*The Connecticut Farmer*, Hartford.

HOW TO DRAW AND PAINT, a neat elementary manual. The little work is illustrated with over one hundred engravings, combining accuracy of detail and excellence of execution. The value of the instructions lies in their simplicity, and the object of the author is well carried out: to afford the beginners such plain directions as may be at once most serviceable, suggestive, and trustworthy.—*New York Star.*

An excellent text-book, containing instruction in outline, light and shade, perspective, sketching, figure drawing, artistic anatomy, landscape, marine, and portrait painting, etc. It also contains over one hundred illustrations.—*The Golden Rule*, Boston, Mass.

For sale by all Booksellers. or will be sent, postpaid, on receipt of price.

EXCELSIOR PUBLISHING HOUSE,

29 and 31 Beekman Street, New York, N. Y.
P. O. Box 1144.

www.ingramcontent.com/pod-product-compliance
Lightning Source LLC
Chambersburg PA
CBHW020016030726
47500CB00002B/619